To Beth [partly covered by barcode label]
my good friends!
Hope you enjoy...

The ACTRESS

Michael Hicks Thompson

SHEPHERD KING PUBLISHING, LLC

4/14/2017

The Actress is a work of fiction. All incidents and dialogue, and all characters are products of the author's imagination and are not to be construed as real.

Bookstores can order from Baker & Taylor.

 SHEPHERD KING PUBLISHING, LLC

2795 Lombardy Avenue
Memphis, TN 38111
michael@shepking.com

ISBN: 978-0-9845282-4-0
ASIN: B01N1O18CH
Library of Congress Control Number: 2016915751
Printed in the United States of America

Author website: **www.michaelthompsonauthor.com**

All scripture quotations are taken from the *NIV Spirit of the Reformation Study Bible*, Copyright © 2003 by Zondervan, Richard L. Pratt, Th.D., General Editor.

Dedication

To my mother,
Olga Wright Thompson,
who could've been a movie star,
but never a diva.

1920 - 1987

Characters in order of appearance:

Martha McRae — *Narrator, Gazette Publisher, boardinghouse owner*

Tully Ivey — *America's most famous actress*

Andrew Dawkins — *Respected local cotton farmer*

Butch Turnbull — *Bethel County sheriff*

Shirley Dawkins — *Wife of Andrew Dawkins*

Randy Carr — *Tully Ivey's agent/attorney*

Andy Chinn — *Movie scriptwriter*

Oneeda Mae Harpole — *Martha's good friend*

Mary Grater — *Martha's friend and boarder; divorced from Capp Grater*

Capp Grater — *Inmate, Parchman Penitentiary*

Alston Goldsmith — *Movie producer, RTO Studios*

Mario Mastrioni — *Actor*

Banner O'Brien — *Movie director*

Father Paul Compañero — *Rector, Calvary Episcopal Church*

Father Adam Davidson — *Former Rector*

Clarence Chapman — *Circuit judge*

Bobby Barrett — *Mississippi governor*

Mike Wood — *Prosecuting attorney*

Frank Acuff — *Defense attorney*

Susie Parker — *Waitress, Charlie's Place diner*

Joanna Whitfield — *Sister of Los Angeles policeman*

A CHRISTIAN MURDER MYSTERY

MICHAEL HICKS THOMPSON

Second in the *Solo* series

[Inspired by a true story]

[The following events take place between August 1962, and September 1963]

To read the short story about my mother, go to Book Fun Magazine *on Amazon, search for the December issue. She was an angel.*

Acknowledgements

To editor Linda Yezak, for saving me from disaster. To Clint Saxton and Thomas Parker, criminal defense attorneys, for editing the courtroom procedures and terminology. To my Beta readers, Dianne Champlin, Roberto Orci, Robbyn Weaver, and Annette Cole Mastron for your sane and valuable input. To Philip Yount and Craig Thompson of Disciple Design for an awesome cover design. And to Michael, Jr., for the cover photography. He's an excellent photographer. To Nick Nixon for the interior images. Well done by all. Thank you.

Here's hoping I didn't leave out a single soul.

Introduction

This story could be told only by me—Martha McRae. I'm the publisher and sole writer for *The Bethel County Gazette*.

I also run a boarding house in Solo, Mississippi. You'll find us on a map in the center of the Delta. Land so level and wide you could see the sun rise on the horizon in the east and set in the west. Cotton and cornfields stretched as far as our eyes could see.

We'd always been a speck of a town, a dot on the map—too small for any stop signs, much less a stoplight. We had a main street, if that's what you wanted to call it. On one side of the train tracks that intersected Solo, you'd recognize five little stores—Insner's Meat Market, Kirk's Feed and Seed, Stegall's General Store, an Esso station, and my Gazette. Tucked away, down a gravel side street was a juke joint.

Walk across the tracks and you'd find Calvary Episcopal Church, a wash-a-mat, a convenience store, and our little post office.

Somehow, Solo seemed to maintain a constant 310 souls. Births replacing deaths.

Deaths. Yes, we had more than our fair share three years ago when Satan paid us a visit. You can read about those murders in *The Rector*.

But here we are again in the land of rich stories and good dirt.

Only this time, there's a celebrity in our midst.

PART I

The Diva

"[He] used fortune-telling and omens and
sorcery, and dealt with mediums
and necromancers.
He did much evil in the sight of the LORD,
provoking him to anger."

— 2 Chronicles 33:6

THE ACTRESS

1
The Intruder

Midnight, August 10, 1962, Solo, Mississippi.

A filthy windowpane separated the most famous actress in America from the human silhouette outside her bedroom.

The crunching of leaves, the sound of footsteps had gotten her attention. She removed her pistol from the bedside drawer and inched her way toward the window. She gathered a breath, then eased a finger to the trigger, pointing the barrel at the dark figure.

The intruder's hand touched the window. She fired. The bullet passed through the glass, into the darkness.

Movie star Tully Ivey had shot local farmer and respected citizen Andrew Dawkins.

The Bethel County Sherriff's Department arrived an hour later. Four Hollywood RTO executives hovered around Dawkins's body. Sheriff Butch Turnbull made a mental note of Tully Ivey crying on a man's shoulder.

Turnbull knelt beside the body and unbuttoned Dawkins's bloody shirt. The bullet wound was dead center chest. Turnbull checked for a pulse. None. He noticed a note clenched in

Dawkins's right hand and a pistol in the grass.

He slipped them both—the gun and the note—into a plastic bag.

The note would hold the key to Tully Ivey's future.

How do I know these things? Because it's my business to know. I'm the only reporter for *The Bethel County Gazette*. The *knowing* is easy. It's the unknown that takes time to uncover.

In a small town like Solo, we know everything about everybody. It's strangers who keep us up at night. And crickets.

I drove to the sheriff's office in Greenlee. Shirley Dawkins had called me, sobbing and hysterical. She needed to know why her husband had been shot and killed. I felt sick for her.

I walked into the sheriff's department at three in the morning. Tully Ivey was sitting across a desk from the sheriff—a hefty man, built like a bull, with a crew cut and bushy eyebrows.

The famous actress was explaining what happened. "He was trying to open the window," she said. "What would you expect me to do?"

She didn't seem the least bit arrogant or irritated. She was calm and collected. I flashed back to her roles on the big screen—elegant, sophisticated, the star of every movie she made.

"It was dark," Butch said. "And the window was dirty. How did you know it was a man?"

Before she could answer, I walked closer. He was surprised to see me. "Martha, what are you doing here? You need to leave."

“I’m here for Shirley. She needs to know what happened.”

Reluctant at first, he nodded in agreement and turned back to Ivey. “So, how did you know it was a man?”

“I didn’t know,” she said. “Like I told you, eventually I went outside to see if someone was still there. I was frightened to death when I discovered his body.”

She looked at *me*. “Wouldn’t you be? *Who* are you?”

I didn’t respond. Maybe I was star-struck.

The sheriff kept probing. “Did you hear him say anything from outside your window? Did he call your name?”

“No, I only heard those crickets. They’re so eerie.”

“You said earlier you hardly knew Mr. Dawkins. Why were you crying over his body?”

“I was upset. Oh, I knew him a little,” she said, squeezing two provocative fingers together like Lauren Bacall. “He had a small role in the movie. I never thought of him as a bad person.”

Butch scratched his cheek. “How do you explain the note? Sure seems like you knew him more than you’re lettin’ on.”

“What note?”

“The note in his hand.”

“Oh, I did notice something in his hand. Was it a note? What did it say?”

Butch took the note from a manila folder. “Here—here’s a copy.”

Tully,

I don't deserve you. I will always love you. I just want you to know the proof of your innoçençe in the Rod Russell shooting is in safe deposit box 4918 at City National Bank. One day I will explain why I didn't tell you earlier. The key is on the ledge.

Andrew

She pressed a hand against her chest. "Oh, my. How did he know I'm innocent of that awful Rod Russell murder?" She expelled a lung of air and placed the note back on Turnbull's desk.

I stepped closer to read it, but he took it away. I could smell her perfume. Tabu.

She reached in her purse and retrieved a thin, silver-engraved box of cigarettes. She selected one and inserted it into a shiny black holder. Deputy Cox, who'd been leaning against the doorjamb, pulled a Zippo from his pocket, strutted over, and lit it. She smiled at him, tossed her head back, and blew out a smoke ring as big as my dinner plates. Cox grinned and dropped the lighter in his trousers, while Butch continued.

"This note says he loves you. Is that why Andrew Dawkins was at your window?"

"I haven't the faintest idea, Sheriff." She batted her Hollywood eyelashes. "Like I told you, I hardly knew him."

"Had he ever been to your window at the Grater house before?"

"Heavens no."

Butch held his palms out to her. "By the way, should I call you Mrs. Ivey?"

"Please, call me Miss Ivey. All my close friends do."

Dropping his head, Butch placed a fist to his mouth and cleared his throat. "I'm not sure you should refer to me as a close friend. Please understand I'm investigating your involvement in a man's death."

"Well okaaay. Ask me anything," she said, casting a polished smile too bright to ignore.

"I should have asked if you'd like to have an attorney present."

Motioning to the man next to her, she said, "Randall Carr here is not only my agent, he's my attorney. He usually lights my cigarettes, too." She sneered at him. "Don't you, Randall?"

Randy Carr was yawning; his chin nestled in his palms. He reached in his pocket, pulled out a butane lighter and flicked it in front of her burning cigarette. She brushed him off and smiled at Deputy Cox, then returned her focus to Butch. "Besides, Sheriff, I don't need a lawyer. He was breaking into my bedroom."

Butch squeezed his eyebrows together. "Did he break the window? Try to open it?"

"I saw a hand. He was trying to break in." She tamped down an unfinished cigarette into the sheriff's tin ashtray.

"Tell me how the pistol ended up beside his body."

"I took it with me. I thought someone might still be outside." A stricken look crossed her face. "Then I saw him on the ground. It was awful. There was blood. He wasn't moving."

Butch kept probing. And Tully Ivey kept repeating the same sequence of events—from when she first saw someone outside, to pulling the trigger.

An hour more of routine questions and the sheriff was done. "I'm going to release you under your own recognizance. But you must not leave Solo without my permission. Do you understand?"

"Of course, Sheriff, whatever you say."

Stamping out her third cigarette, she stood, as tall and regal as her reputation. She oozed grace and charm with the confidence of royalty who'd never expected to spend a single night in some Mississippi jail cell.

Butch seemed enamored with her. Me? I was disappointed in the sheriff's interrogation.

"Cox, I want you to drive Miz Ivey and Mr. Carr out to the Grater house," the sheriff said.

"Be my pleasure," Cox said, spreading his cowboy legs, both thumbs wrapped around his belt buckle.

After Tully Ivey and Randy Carr left with Deputy Cox, I approached the sheriff, "How come you let her off so easy?"

His response was lame. "If somebody was trying to get into your bedroom in the middle of the night what would you do?"

"I'd call you."

He scowled. "Martha, I'd advise you not to get involved in this."

"It's too late. I'm doing this for Shirley."

He walked away in a huff.

And it was too late to visit Shirley, so I phoned her from the sheriff's department.

"Shirley, I am so sorry about Andrew. I believe it was just a terrible accident."

I explained some of the circumstances, but didn't mention the note. No sense rattling her nerves more than necessary.

"But, Martha, what was Andrew doing at her window? Why was he there?"

"I don't know. But I'm going to look into it." She deserved to know why her husband died.

"You will? Thank you. Thank you so much." Her voice broke on a sob.

Driving home, I vowed to root out any evil behind his death—if there was any. Maybe the shooting was self-defense. In the Mississippi Delta, we're not sure who committed anything. Including murders. Maybe Tully Ivey had every right to shoot somebody breaking into her bedroom.

We all knew Andrew Dawkins as a good-looking, well-respected cotton farmer in Bethel County. Two years ago, we even thought he might marry Mary Grater after her divorce from Capp. But one day—*whoosh!*—he was gone. Turned up a month later with Shirley Williamson from Memphis on his arm. He stayed out on his farm and did his churching—and everything else—in Greenlee, probably because he was too embarrassed to face our little Bible study group at church on Sundays.

Shirley Dawkins was his opposite. If Calvary's doors were open, she was there. Mary and Shirley even became good friends in our Bible study group. I always thought it was very Christian-like, Mary holding no grudges against Shirley and all.

Still, the note in Andrew's hand led to a series of bizarre discoveries nobody expected.

2
The Movie

Hollywood moviemakers come to the Mississippi Delta in search of dirt-rich, titillating stories. Stories from Tennessee Williams, William Faulkner, and now me, Martha McRae.

I'm just a small-town widow surviving on a ragtag weekly newspaper, a boardinghouse, and a book I'd written about the good people of Solo—and the evil that had taken root in our little speck of Delta earth.

I soon learned "Hollywood" had come to exploit the evil in my book, not the good.

When RTO Studios first contacted me, I was floored. They wanted to make a movie out of *The Rector*.

"How much do you pay for something like that?"

"Mrs. McRae, I'm authorized to offer you $25,000."

More than I make in two years.

The deal went through and I deposited the check in Greenlee's Bank Plus branch.

Within a few weeks, a location scout rented one of my rooms. He spent two weeks taking photographs around Bethel County.

Two months later, the film crew arrived.

Most of the regular crew—soundman, cameraman, grips, makeup people—stayed at the new Holiday Inn in Greenlee. But the movie's producer rented the Grater house for the executive crew and lead actors, Tully Ivey and Mario Mastrioni.

I was surprised to hear Capp Grater had rented his home. Oneeda claimed he "needed the money." Whatever for, I'll never know, as he'd likely fade away in prison. Two years ago, Capp had to abandon Solo's largest and grandest home in exchange for a ten-foot cell in Parchman Penitentiary.

I helped put him away.

The Grater home had been decked out with exotic species of hardwoods—Brazilian Cherry, tiger maple, even some African species I could never pronounce—all courtesy of Capp's lumber business.

Capp had built a Southern-style, five-bedroom mansion with a commercial kitchen, a burl walnut paneled library, and a garden room—my favorite. It was filled with indigenous plants that grow more lush than stories told at Delta cocktail parties.

Five of the RTO executives slept upstairs—Al Goldsmith, the producer; Banner O'Brien, the director; Mario Mastrioni, the lead male actor; and Randy Carr. Tully Ivey had the downstairs master bedroom.

The young scriptwriter, Andy Chinn, rented one of my upstairs rooms. "For peace and quiet," he'd said, "where I can think and write. No distractions."

At night, Chinn always went out drinking with the crew. On

one such occasion, Oneeda Mae Harpole, my best friend and Solo's busiest gossip, snuck into Chinn's room and found the movie script. After reading part of it, she met me downstairs with the news.

"Martha, it's about capital punishment. About Mississippi—how immoral we are for executing Sonny Sartain."

"Sonny Sartain? A movie about *him*?"

I'd been a witness at his execution. If he wasn't Lucifer's brother, he was next of kin.

"*The Killing*. That's the name of the movie," Oneeda added.

"And all this time I thought it was gonna be a decent movie about Father Davidson," I said, disappointed.

"The producer, Al Goldsmith—remember what he told us in church? He said it was gonna be about Davidson." With a sad face, Oneeda added, "They've stopped filming for now, though."

"I know. The tabloids ran a story about it."

"What'd it say?"

"I have it here somewhere. Let me find it." I grabbed it from my nightstand and returned.

"Here it is," I said." I'll read it. Goldsmith says, 'We decided to stop production until our star feels up to being back on camera, after such an ordeal.' Is that not the sorriest excuse you've ever heard?" I slapped the magazine against my palm and smiled. "But he can't be a happy man right now. I read somewhere that every day lost in the movie business is money down the drain."

3
Miss Ivey

Tallulah Ivey is her real name. But her stage name is Tully Ivey. Anybody who's been in a movie theater knows her—or at least knows her screen image. Those closest to her, the ones who attend to her every whim, call her "Miss Ivey." She's single (divorced three times) and rarely without Randy Carr by her side.

Carr, a full-blooded American capitalist, accumulated as much capital as possible from Tully Ivey's stardom—not a trial lawyer, just her agent-lawyer, running interference on legal matters for ten-percent of her earnings. He reminded me of a bird with specs. Tall and skinny, balding, with circular wire-rim glasses clinging to a beak-nose.

My first clue in Andrew Dawkins's death came on August four, a week *before* the shooting. Oneeda had visited to drop off some gossip. It was a Sunday afternoon.

Smacking on her Juicy Fruit, she said, "Guess who Susie Parker saw last night? Andrew Dawkins, with that movie actress, Tully Ivey. I think they've got something goin' on."

"Goin' on? Whadda you mean?"

"You know," she wiggled her brows, "between the sheets."

“Really? How do you know?”

“Remember, it rained yesterday. They shut down filming. Everybody took the day off. Tully Ivey and Andrew ate supper at Charlie’s Place. Susie was their waitress. She waited on Tully Ivey! Can you believe it? And Andrew... he’s playing a small role in the movie. That’s how he got to know her.”

“So? Maybe they were discussing the script.”

“Nope. Susie says she overheard ’em talking about meeting up. She didn’t hear everything, but she heard Tully Ivey say, ‘meet at the Alamo tonight.’”

“The Alamo Motel?”

Oneeda’s face wrinkled into a frown. “I know. It’s turned into a one-hour sinning service.”

Three days after the shooting, we buried Andrew Dawkins. I sat between Mary and Oneeda on the second row, unable to keep my eyes off grieving widow Shirley Dawkins. She sat on Calvary’s front pew—dabbing her eyes with a linen handkerchief.

Father Paul Compañero, one of my boarders, performed the service. With solemn eyes he acknowledged the congregation.

“The passing of a loved one leaves a hole in our heart. We miss them. But death is inevitable, is it not? Yet, our souls live on for eternity. Where our souls go from here is more important than the life we lived on earth. But Andrew Dawkins lived a good life. He was a man of faith. And right now he’s in a far better place.”

Blah, blah, blah …

Ahh, funerals. The preacher always says the same thing—*He lived a good life. He's in heaven now.*

If only that last part were always true.

Like any minister with concern for the grieving, Father Compañero leaned over the pulpit and addressed the widow.

"Shirley, while Andrew's obedience to God may have lapsed, and though his faith may have weakened, Jesus remained faithful to him."

Shirley bawled, while we dabbed our eyes.

Father Compañero limped down two sanctuary steps toward Shirley. (Father Paul wore a right leg brace, having contracted polio as a five-year-old growing up poor in Mexico.)

She looked up at him as he leaned down and held her hands. We could hear him. "Shirley, trust in the Lord. I want to meet with you next week. I have a book on grief. It will help you."

She could only nod.

Later, at the gravesite, I spotted Tully Ivey. She must've been hiding in the back of the nave during the church service. Out in the open, she was the obvious starlet—tight black sequined dress and dark sunglasses surrounding her eyes like a woman born out of mystery. Her dark red hair added to her intrigue. And why not? She was the queen of glamour. I'll admit, the stories Oneeda had told me were titillating.

For some odd, truthful reason, hearing about somebody else's glamorous life can transport me from my little world into their exciting one. But only for the glamour part, not the dirt. Was I wrong to have those thoughts?

Sheriff Turnbull and the movie star stepped off to the side to talk. Oneeda and I walked toward them, close enough to eavesdrop.

"I just have a few more questions to ask," he said to Ivey.

She lowered her head and sunglasses a tad. Her cold eyes telegraphed disdain. Such a wicked look even I withered.

Butch said, "That's okay. I suppose it can wait'll next week."

After we passed them, Oneeda and I turned back to look.

The queen of opulence didn't say a word to the sheriff. She simply took Randy Carr's arm and marched into the fellowship hall.

"Oneeda, you go on ahead, I'll catch up later."

I approached the awe-struck sheriff. "Why is she even here? Shouldn't she be in custody?"

Removing his lingering attention from her, he focused his narrow eyes on me. "Do *what?*"

"Don't you need the DA or judge's approval to release her?"

"Leave it alone, Martha." Butch Turnbull walked away with one parting remark tossed over his shoulder. "And no, I don't need a judge or DA's permission."

"I think you have celebrityitis," I said to his back.

He spun around and scowled. "I have what?"

"I think you're star-struck." I closed the space between us. "Look, Butch, I'll make a trade with you. I won't write a word about this in the *Gazette* if you'll let me make a copy of the note you found in Andrew's hand."

He stepped directly in front of me. His face glistened with perspiration from the hot August day.

"Not a chance. That note is department evidence." He hitched up his pants and planted both hands on large hips. "Are you trying to blackmail me?"

"It's not blackmail. It's white mail. As in newspaper white. I'm gonna write about it in the *Gazette*." I propped my hands on my hips to match his. "Butch, I'm a reporter, remember?"

"I think—I think… meet me at my office tomorrow morning, eight sharp." Twirling his large frame around, he stormed off, this time wiping his forehead with a red bandanna.

I didn't care if he was mad. I'd get a copy of the note tomorrow.

Once again, reporters descended upon the Delta. And why not? This was Tully Ivey, America's sweetheart.

The Los Angeles Times, the *New York Post*, Salem's *Clarion-Ledger*, the Hollywood tabloids—they came from everywhere, just in time for Dawkins's funeral and "after" lunch in Calvary's fellowship hall. The reporters re-acquainted like buzzards over tuna salad, potato salad, and too many casseroles to count. But it was our skillet fried chicken that had them salivating.

Standing behind the food table, Randy Carr used a spoon to tinkle his glass and get everyone's attention. Tully Ivey stood next to him. We all gaped at her.

I couldn't believe she had the nerve to be there.

She waited until the room was silent. "Thank you, Randall," she said, then paused to study her audience.

"I sincerely hope all of you understand this terrible tragedy was an accident. *Truly an accident.* I am so sorry about Mr. Dawkins and sorry I was the one who had to pull that awful trigger. I wish it had been somebody else."

Low ceilings in our fellowship hall gave her voice so much presence the crowd hung on every word.

"My new friends, I wish to put this unfortunate tragedy behind me. Will you do that with me? Can we put this terrible accident behind us and move on? Move on with our lives." She touched a tissue to her eye. "I—I don't know what else to say."

With one eye barely open and an index finger wiping a tear from the other, she paused to peek at her audience. "Now … I will say, though, this Southern food of yours is simply divine. I just love the South."

Somebody clapped, then another and another. It was easy to forget we were attending a funeral.

She wasn't finished. She placed one hand to her throat and waved the other over the food-laden table. "Why, I never taste delicacies like this in Hollywood."

Many in the crowd smiled and whispered about her sincere remorse. I probably wasn't the only one who thought it was all phony baloney.

There must've been a hundred folks there, maybe more; half seemed to be vying for a close encounter with the diva. I understood the fascination with celebrities. But at a funeral?

Oneeda took my hand and said, "Come on, we're going to meet her."

"I don't need to meet her. I met her at the police station. Besides, we should be mourning Andrew's death. Frankly, I can't believe she's even here."

"Don't be such a pill, this is different."She grabbed my arm and dragged me through the admirers.

We were introduced. "Yes, I remember you," Ivey said. "You were at the sheriff's department the other night."

"I was."

Before I could say another word, reporters had rooted their way through the crowd. Randy Carr placed a chicken wing in her hand. She posed like a fashion model. Flashbulbs began popping. They all wanted an image of her eating our Southern food.

Oneeda and I were squeezed to the back of the circle.

"You can stay if you want, but I'm leaving."

"Don't go. She won't be tied up for long. Let's eat something and come back."

"I'm not hungry. Besides, I need to finish Andrew's obituary."

"I thought you'd written it."

"Not yet. Look, I'll see you later, okay?" When I turned to leave, I felt a prick at the back of my head. It was my hatpin. It was too long for the hat I wore; but it was the only one I could find that morning. I shoved it in my purse, then dug out my keys.

As I walked away, Oneeda waved bye, then began pushing her way through the crowd toward the diva. Shirley Dawkins came out of nowhere and grabbed hold of Oneeda's skirt, using her for interference. They inched their way through the crowd. I stopped to watch.

Shirley was a shrimp of a thing. Her red eyes and dark circles suggested she'd been crying for days. And she was about to meet the woman who'd shot and killed her husband. I wasn't about to miss this.

I lost sight of them, so I did what I had to—I stood on a chair.

She broke away from Oneeda and stumbled into the movie star's arms. Shirley straightened up and delivered a walloping smack across Ivey's left cheek. The crowd hushed. Two women kept Shirley from crumpling to the floor.

Unfazed, Tully Ivey placed a palm on her cheek. "How thoughtful of you, my dear. I do believe I missed an application of rouge this morning. Right here, on the left. Would you gentlemen take a portrait of me? I'd like to see if the color on both sides matches now." She exhibited her best camera pose. The photographers ate it up.

When the flashbulbs stopped, she looked at Shirley. "Darling, you must be the wife. I am deeply sorry for what happened. But, dear, it was an accident."

Shirley twirled and lurched back through the crowd. People helped her to the outside ring of on-lookers. Oneeda grabbed her and they left through the kitchen's back door.

I met them outside. Oneeda was holding Shirley up, keeping her from falling to the ground.

"Oh, Shirley, I am so sorry," I said. "Oneeda, how can I help?"

"I'm going to take her home. I'll stay with her. We'll be all right. Catch up with you tomorrow."

Shirley wouldn't stop sobbing. Looking up to the sky and back to the ground, she kept asking, "Why? Why was Andrew there, Lord?"

On the white rock road, Ivy's black sedan serpentined between the granite headstones, home to hundreds of Calvary's long forgotten.

The next day, I drove to the sheriff's department in Greenlee, ready to get my copy of the note Andrew had in his hand. Sheriff Turnbull handed me the original, secured in a plastic evidence bag, but I could read every word.

Tully,

I don't deserve you. I will always love you. I just want you to know the proof of your innoçençe in the Rod Russell shooting is in safe deposit box 4918 at City National Bank. One day I will explain why I didn't tell you earlier. The key is on the ledge.

Andrew

Hmmm, seemed Andrew may have loved her after all. But what was this Rod Russell shooting about?

Sheriff Turnbull took the note away and interrupted my thought with the same question. "What in tarnation is this Russell shooting about?" He wasn't speaking to me, just thinking out loud. "It makes no sense. What would Andrew Dawkins know about her shooting some man in Los Angeles?"

"The note mentions some key to a lockbox," I said. "The answer is in there. We need see what's in that lockbox."

"There's no *we* here, Martha. I give the orders. And you're not involved. Besides, there ain't no key."

"On the ledge. Right there in the note. It says he left a key on the ledge."

"We searched for hours. There was no key."

"What about his pockets?"

"Look at me. We searched his pockets. We had four men scour the entire area for three hours. They found nothing. Now, you have to understand, this is a police matter. You are not part of this department. We'll take it from here." He dropped the note on his desk and turned to walk away.

I looked closer at the note. "Wait, Butch. Why is there tape on the note? Did you put it there?"

"No. I figured Dawkins never had a chance to tape it to the window."

I picked it up again, studied it. "Look, this is odd. The tape is on the wrong side of the note. Why would he leave a note for her to read if he taped it facing outward? He would have placed the tape on the backside of the note, so she could read it from inside the house. The tape is on the wrong side."

"What? Let me see."

Taking the note, he flipped it again and again, studying the tape. "You're right. The note was intended to be taped on the window so it showed out, not in."

"Did you check it for fingerprints?"

"Why would I? It was his note."

"You should check it for prints. I would."

"So you're a detective now, huh?"

"Maybe I should be."

If I were on the inside of this investigation, I could learn a lot more.

"Look, I'll make you another deal. Deputize me and I won't write a story about this note in the *Gazette*."

"Again? You're trying to blackmail me again? I have a mind to—"

"Call it what you want—blackmail, white mail, I don't care. Do it. Make me a deputy."

He tossed his straw hat on the desk and eased a hand through his crew cut. "Martha, Martha, I appreciate everything you did to help three years ago, but you know I can't make you a deputy. It's not possible."

"Butch, if there's one thing I know you can do, it's deputize a citizen who can help. Says so in Mississippi law and you know it. 'In times of crisis a sheriff can appoint deputies.'"

"Right. In times of *crisis*."

"What do you think this is?"

"This is not a crisis," he said.

"Oh, but it is. I bet there's going to be another murder."

"Your instincts again? Riiight." His voice dripped with sarcasm. "And you'd be the only deputy in the history of Mississippi—maybe even America—who got their badge based on *instincts*."

"My instincts helped get you re-elected. Remember?"

He leaned over and planted both fists firmly on top of his desk. He couldn't stop shaking his head. His face telegraphed resignation.

Butch Turnbull and I had been friends—well, sort of friends—

since I helped him pin a murder on Capp Grater three years ago. It practically assured his re-election. He owed me for that.

Deputizing me took only ten minutes. I simply repeated the Deputy Oath. *Do no harm, save lives*, those sorts of things.

"Do I have to wear a deputy uniform?"

"I wouldn't give you a uniform if you wanted it," he said. "Everybody in Bethel County is gonna think I lost my mind. And I don't want you wearing the badge, either. Keep it in your purse. And no weapon."

"I don't want a weapon."

"One more thing. I want you to report to me every day. No, make it two times a day. Noon and five. Swear to me you'll do it."

"You have my word. Should I call you *sir* now?"

He gave me a serious I'm-not-even-gonna-answer-that look.

"Okay, noon and five. But you owe me something."

He plopped back in his chair, looked up at the ceiling, and sighed. "What could I possibly owe you now?"

"You promised me a copy of the note, remember?"

"I'm about to change my mind."

"I just need a copy. You keep the original."

"Martha!" Oneeda squealed, staring at my shiny badge. "You really *are* a detective."

"I'm a deputy sheriff, not a detective."

"Still, you're official. How'd you ever get Turnbull to agree?"

"I'll tell you later. Look at this. It's a copy of the note Andrew had in his hand."

Oneeda studied it. "Goodness. Says he *loves* her. And this Russell shooting… what's that about? This is really strange."

"I know. I've got to get in that lockbox."

"Won't the sheriff do that?"

"You reminded me—it's after five. I'm supposed to call him twice a day. He's very strict."

I rang him. "Sheriff, this is Martha."

"It's five thirty. You're late."

"Sorry. Listen, Butch, have you figured out where the lockbox is—which bank it's in?"

"Working on it. Look, I have an assignment for you. I want you to go to the high school tomorrow and check on an incident down there. Got a complaint about some McAllister kid. Seems he started a brawl on the football field. And his nose is broken. Get me your report as soon as possible."

"Solo High School? Is that what I'm gonna be doing, working school detail?"

"I give the assignments, Martha. Understood?"

"Yessir."

I hung up, so mad my ears were burning. Oneeda was standing beside me, chewing her Juicy Fruit. "He wants me to investigate some high school thing. He wants to remove me from this investigation. I don't like it, Oneeda. I wanna see this through for Shirley, not stuck on some school duty."

I had already planned to use my new deputy status to get inside that lockbox—most likely, in City National's main branch in Salem, the capital of Mississippi. That's where most folks would keep their prized possessions. I just knew Butch was gonna figure it out and open the lockbox *without* me.

"I have an idea," Oneeda said.

We talked. Seemed like a decent plan. Tricky, but doable.

4
The Badge

I snapped a Polaroid of my badge, let it dry, then carefully cut out the main image and pressed it firm over my real badge to give it a 3-dimensional look. I glued some cotton swabs under the photo and stuck it on the inside of my late husband's old wallet. Oneeda could use it to fake her way into the school and ask questions. She was a good egg for doing this.

"You'll have to flash it quickly, so nobody gets a good look at it," I said.

"I know. They all know me at school. I'll tell 'em I've been deputized," she said, casting a wide smile.

The next morning, I left for Salem, for City National's main branch, hoping, praying Butch would never know.

Two and a half hours later, I walked into the bank. After presenting my badge to a woman behind a desk, I said, "Yes, ma'am, official business. I need to get into lockbox 4918. It involves a possible murder."

Wasn't sure if she believed me or not, but she rang the manager.

A tidy-looking man approached. He reeked of Old Spice. "Ma'am, you say you want us to open deposit box number 4918?"

"Yes, I do. Official business." I flashed my badge again. "There's been a shooting."

"May I ask why you would want to open the governor's deposit box?"

My heart skipped a beat. "The governor's box?"

"Correct," he said, not a single movement in his taut face.

"I—I, there must be some mistake. Lockbox 4918 can't be the governor's."

"Deputy… I'm sorry, I didn't get your name."

"Deputy McRae," I said, barely able to get it out. Oh, boy, I'm going to be in trouble with Butch.

"Sir, I think I may be in the wrong bank. My sincere apologies."

"Accepted, Deputy. Have a nice day." He twirled around and marched away.

Me? I slinked out onto the street. Butch is gonna scorch me to a cinder when he hears about this. I paced to my car and drove back to Solo. I had only two things on my mind—praying Butch wouldn't take away my badge, and wondering how the governor could possibly be mixed up in this.

The answers would come later.

A week passed, and still no scorching from Butch. He must not've heard about my visit to Salem. Thank goodness.

5
Mary & Paul

Mary Grater had continued to stay with me, not wanting to be in the big Grater house alone with a young boy. She'd been through a lot, but she hadn't changed an iota. She was still as pretty and kind as ever.

On the afternoon of September ten, I fixed supper for her, little Michael, and Father Compañero. It was my first attempt at Mexican food. I wanted to cook something special for Father Paul. Mary helped.

Without Andy Chinn there, we felt free to talk about the movie script and how awful it would make Mississippians look.

Mississippi already had its fair share of negative publicity, what with the Ole Miss riots a few weeks ago. Segregationists were still protesting the enrollment of James Meredith, a black military veteran. Two civilians and a French journalist had been killed. The negative stories would set us back for years.

"I don't get this segregation thing," Father Paul said. "Why are those students so determined to keep somebody with a different color skin out of their school?"

"Most Mississippians are perfectly happy with the governor's stance," I said. "I just hope the next generation will right the wrongs and restore our image. But if RTO Studios has their way with that awful script, it'll be an uphill battle."

Everybody agreed.

After supper, Mary put Michael to bed, while Father Paul helped with the dirty dishes. "Martha, tell me what's going on with you. You look worried about something."

Father Compañero reminded me so much of Father Adam Davidson—big, earnest eyes made everyone feel like they were the only person he cared about.

"Oh, I'm not worried," I said. "Just trying to concentrate and figure things out."

"You're still pursuing the Dawkins shooting?"

"I am."

"Tell me about it."

I removed my apron. We sat at my favorite spot—the kitchen table. Close by, my vintage motor-top refrigerator generated an unrelenting hum, and the cabinets craved for a fresh coat of Kelly Green paint.

Father Paul and I drank coffee while I told him everything—from the governor's lockbox to Dawkins and Ivey's rumored tryst. All of it.

"Martha, I'm concerned for you. I hope you won't mind me asking, but are you sure you're qualified to investigate this?"

"Father, if you'd been here three years ago when I helped Butch make those arrests, you wouldn't be saying that. I have a perfectly *fine* nose for this."

"I'm just saying, be careful."

We finished, and said our good nights.

Next morning, I woke with a burning question—why hasn't Butch made more progress? He'd gotten nowhere. He'd already questioned the movie executives about the missing key. Maybe I should interview them.

6
Official Business

The Grater property looked like Vicksburg's *Castle Hill* after the Civil War—overgrown weeds and grass, out of control rose bushes, and windows that surely hadn't been cleaned since Capp took up residence in Parchman.

I knocked on the door.

Andy Chinn, the scriptwriter and one of my boarders, answered. He seemed startled to see me. "Oh, hello, Mrs. McRae. I didn't expect you here."

"I'm the new deputy. I'm here on official business." I presented my badge. "I'd like to ask you all some questions. May I come in?"

"Of course. I didn't know you were a deputy."

"Just yesterday."

He glanced over his shoulder like he expected to see someone behind him. He seemed tense.

To make him feel at ease, I said, "I can hear you typing upstairs at my place."

"I hope it doesn't keep you up at night."

"No, it's sort of rhythmic, all that tap-tap-taping with whatever you're writing."

Walking into the center of the marble foyer, he said,

"Yep, I'm the one who comes up with all those gruesome murder scenes."

He must've noticed my surprised look.

"It's a joke," he said, smiling. "Would you like me to gather the others?"

"Yes, thank you."

He bounded up the stairs. He was over six feet tall, muscular and dark complexioned. Had to be a California tan, though I'd never seen one in person. The blonde hair reminded me of Tab Hunter.

The place was filthy. Dust clouded everything—the floors, walls, paintings; even the chandelier had lost its luster.

I walked into the library. The furniture was wrapped in a milky white plastic, with one exception. Immediately inside the room was a high-back wingchair covered in a black and gold paisley print. I brushed my palm over it. It felt expensive. Next to the chair was a side table with an ashtray full of cigarette butts and some strange-looking, elaborately illustrated cards placed in neat rows. They were the size of bridge cards. I'd never seen anything like them.

Andy Chinn walked in with three other men. He introduced me to Randy Carr, Banner O'Brien, and Mario Mastrioni—whom I recognized from his movies. Handsome, but only about five-foot-six, which surprised me. There was no mistaking his Italian heritage, though.

"Where are Tully Ivey and Mr. Goldsmith?"

"They're both in L.A.," O'Brien said.

"But they're coming back, right?"

They all glanced at each other. "Yes, of course," O'Brien answered.

"Does Sheriff Turnbull know she left Mississippi?"

"Of course. We would never dream of breaking Sheriff Turnbull's rules," a syrupy Randy Carr said, and added, "You were there at the Sheriff's department when he questioned Miss Ivey, weren't you?"

"Yes, I was. When do you expect them back?"

O'Brien answered, "We have no idea, Deputy. Really, we don't".

Banner O'Brien seemed like the nice one in the bunch.

I suggested we all take a seat. Three of us settled on plastic-covered furniture while Mastrioni stood by the boarded-up fireplace. Chinn sat behind the desk in another plastic chair. Nobody sat in the wingback. I wrote all their names and titles in my notebook, and took shorthand of everything said. I didn't want to broach the "key" subject right away, so I eased into it.

"Which one of you came outside first, after the shooting?"

"There were three of us initially—myself, Al, and Mario," O'Brien said, then pointed to Randy Carr. "Randy says he never heard the gunshot. He showed up later."

"When you got to the scene, Mr. O'Brien, what was Mrs. Ivey doing?"

"She was down on the ground, hugging the body, and crying. I don't think any of us realized they knew each other that well. She must've liked him an awful lot."

"Andy, when did you wake up and go down?"

"I was at your place. Remember?"

"Oh, right." I smiled and addressed Mastrioni. "Was she crying when you got there?"

"Yes, she was crying."

"Did she say anything? Anything at all?"

"I heard her say, 'Oh, Andrew, what have I done?'" Mastrioni turned to face O'Brien. "But Banner is mistaken. I don't think they knew each other that well."

Andy Chinn piped up. "Aww, that's bunk, Mario, and you know it. Tully fell for every good-looking pair of pants she ever met. Admit it."

Nobody uttered a word.

I broke the silence. "Andy, that seems mighty harsh. Do you have a problem with her?"

"Heavens no. I just stay out of her way. Always thought she was trouble. Why do you think I rented from you?"

That was odd. He'd told me it was for peace and quiet. "You said she's *trouble*. What do you mean?"

"Let's just say she could absorb anyone she wanted."

He had my attention now. “Explain what you mean, *absorb anyone*.”

“She owned you. The men close to her became like putty in her hands, doing whatever she wanted. I saw it more times than I can count.”

“Do all of you feel the same way about her?”

“No, not me. We’re fine together,” Mastrioni said, shooting a dagger at Chinn.

“I’m sure you are,” Chinn said, sarcasm in his voice.

I jumped in. “The sheriff said when he got here she was crying on somebody’s shoulder.”

Mastrioni spoke up. “Mine.”

I shifted in my chair. “Did any of you go to the window and look around?”

“Look around?” Mastrioni cocked an eyebrow.“What for?”

Leaning forward, I said, “Okay, I’ll get to the point. Which one of you found the key on the ledge?”

O’Brien shrugged. “We don’t know anything about a key. The Sheriff asked us the same question.”

“I didn’t see any key,” Mastrioni said. “I never went near the window. I was barefooted. There was glass on the ground.”

“Me too. Barefooted,” O’Brien said.

“What about Mr. Goldsmith?”

"I don't remember him saying anything about a key," O'Brien said.

"Wait, *none* of you noticed a key on the ledge?"

They all shook their heads.

"What kind of key was it?" Chinn wanted to know. "What's it unlock?"

"I'm not at liberty to say."

At that point, I never expected any of them would confess to having the key.

I stood. "Gentlemen, thank you for your time. Here's my phone number if you think of anything else."

I drove back to town, hoping Butch didn't bawl me out for that impromptu—and fruitless—interview. I'd long since stopped calling Butch twice a day. Not even once a day. He must've had too many things on his plate to worry about me.

Father Compañero, Mary, and I were in the kitchen when Oneeda showed up with her version of the school incident.

Sitting beside me she said, "That McAllister boy, he's a mean one."

"What happened? Don't leave anything out. I need it for my report."

"Oh, it was a big fight. The coach had issued all the football equipment to the team. This new boy from Catfish Point, Ben 'Chunky' Lungren, had never seen football equipment in his life. He asked about an equipment item—one of those athletic supporters the boys wear to protect… you know, their privates. Shane McAllister thought he'd play a joke on this new kid. McAllister told him it was a nose guard. Lungren was the last one to come trottin' out on the field. The athletic supporter was strapped around his forehead with the pouch thing covering his nose."

Father Paul's eyes popped open, while Mary and I laughed till we cried.

"Yep, all those boys laughed, too," Oneeda said. "The coach even had a chuckle."

Mary couldn't stop laughing. "So… what happened next?"

"Lungren asked all the boys where *their* nose guards were. McAllister called him a 'fool'. Then Lungren said, 'You ain't supposed to call nobody a fool accordin' to the Bible.' So he knocked the tar out of the McAllister boy. Broke his nose."

"Ouch," Father Paul said.

"Yep, that's when the fight broke out. Evidently, half the boys liked Lungren and took up for him. According to the coach, it was an ugly fight. McAllister's parents called in the complaint. But everything's back to normal now. That's my report, Deputy McRae."

I smiled at her delusion of being a real deputy. "That's enough detail for *my* report," I said, still smiling.

"There's a moral to this story," Father Paul said.

We waited to hear it.

"The only time you should look down your nose is when you're helping someone up."

We all nodded.

Returning to the *Gazette* the next day, I began my ritual of calling advertisers to thank them and ask about next week's ad. Without them I wouldn't be in business.

Afterwards, I sat at my typewriter, eager to write about the shooting. But I had writer's block. I picked up the note and read it again for inspiration. That's when I noticed the letter c in "innoçençe." It had a flaw. It looked like a piece of metal had stuck to the bottom of the c. A manufacturing flaw. How could I have missed it? It was definitely a ç. And the only çs in the entire note were in the word innoçençe. Odd.

At supper, I showed the note to Mary and Father Paul. Mary wanted to know what I thought of it.

"I don't know yet. I have to visit Shirley and type the letter c on Andrew's typewriter. Let's hope it matches, so this whole mess will be over. Except for the lockbox. We still need to find out what's in there."

"What if it *wasn't* typed on Andrew's typewriter?" Father Paul asked.

"Then we'll be pretty sure he didn't type it," I said with a straight face.

"And there's the note in the lockbox," Mary said.

“It might belong to the governor. I’m not sure what to do.”

“The governor? That’s got to be a coincidence,” she said.

“You know I don’t believe in coincidences.”

Shirley opened her front door, her eyes still wet from the loss of her husband.

“Come in, please.” We stood in the doorway.

“Shirley, I am so sorry about what happened. Is there anything I can do for you?”

“Just pray. And thank you for going to the sheriff’s office.” She dabbed her eyes with a tissue. “I still don’t understand any of this, Martha. It’s just so… like a bad dream.” She looked at me.“Did you find out why Andrew was at that woman’s window?”

“I have something you need to see.”

“What? What is it?”

“Let’s have a seat. I’ll show you.”

We sat beside each other of the sofa. I handed her my copy of the note.

She read it and cried. “How could he? How could he?”

I patted her hand until she settled down. Softly, I said, “I need to check Andrew’s typewriter.”

Hope sparked in her eyes. “You think there’s a chance he didn’t type the note?”

“It would mean a lot if he didn’t.”

She escorted me to Andrew's back office—a large Quonset hut full of farm implements, welding equipment, and tools everywhere. Scattered on a large table in the middle, were farming magazines, dirty coffee mugs, and plenty of mess. A Royal typewriter was in the center.

I sat in Andrew's old chair, behind the typewriter. "I'd like to put in some paper and type something."

"Of course." She hurried to grab a blank sheet from the drawer. "Here, use this."

While I rolled in the paper, she took the note from the desk and studied it again. "Lord, I pray he didn't type this note."

Suddenly, she shoved it in my line of sight, jabbing it with a finger. "Look, he didn't sign it. Why would someone type their name and not sign it?"

"I'm not sure. Maybe he was in a hurry."

I hit the c key several times, then bent over for an inspection. Perfect. No flaws. "Andrew didn't type the note," I said, "unless he used some other typewriter. Are there any others?"

"No. Only this one. That's good news, right?"

"I think so. But it adds a new wrinkle."

"Whadda you mean?"

"Think about it. Suppose Andrew didn't type the note. Why was it in his hand?"

"I don't know. You'll find out, won't you, Martha?" Her eyes brimmed with tears.

7
The Producer

It was time to bring the sheriff in on the ç discovery.

He was busy. I waited in the breakroom. When he showed up with an empty mug, I held out my copy of the note.

"Butch, have you noticed these çs in the word innoçençe?"

"Yeah, I saw that yesterday. What about it?"

"I think you should take some men out to the Grater house and check their typewriters. One of 'ems bound to have this ç."

"No. First, we're gonna check Dawkins's typewriter."

He picked up the Dawkins note to study it again.

"Well, that's sorta already been checked," I said, "The note isn't from his typewriter."

His face became red, same as always when mad. He tossed the note on the counter.

"You've been out to see Shirley Dawkins without my permission, haven't you?" He scowled, grabbed the note, and walked away.

I followed him to his office.

"You were supposed to take care of the school problem," he added.

"It's taken care of, Butch. Everything's back to normal."

"Oh, really? Okay, let me think. You haven't written a report on the school incident, yet you had time to visit Shirley Dawkins. How'd you manage all that?"

"My report is … well, I'm almost finished with it."

"Today would be good."

I nodded.

He walked to the window and gazed outside, thinking.

Eventually, he turned to me. "You say it's not Dawkins's typewriter. You're sure?"

"Yessir."

"One member of the film crew is boarding with you, right?"

"Andy Chinn, the scriptwriter. But the note didn't come from his typewriter, either."

"So you've checked it, too?"

"Yessir."

He sighed. "Well, that just leaves the typewriters out at the Grater house." Butch had interviewed them in department headquarters; all except Al Goldsmith, who'd been in California.

"There're five of 'em," I blurted, then wanted to slap a hand over my big mouth.

He landed in the chair behind his desk. "How do you know there're five of 'em?"

My hesitation probably made me look sheepish. His scowl

changed to sadness. "Martha, Martha, don't tell me you've been out there, *too*?"

"Butch, you had a closed mind about all this. It's more than self-defense. I can sense it."

"What, your intuition again?"

"It hasn't failed me yet and you know it."

He huffed and walked to the window again. "Maybe you're right. I'll take some men out there. We'll check their typewriters."

"I've met most of 'em. I need to go with you."

He turned around to face me, put his hands on his hips, and squinted fiery blue eyes at me, not saying a word.

"I can help, Butch. I promise, I won't get in the way."

Two-thirty in the afternoon, three squad cars eased up to the Grater house. Five of us deputies approached the front door.

The movie director, O'Brien, met us and yelled upstairs, "Mr. Goldsmith, perhaps you should come down. Some police officers are here."

Once inside, I peeked into the library. Tully Ivey was sitting in the wingback chair, reading a stack of papers, not moving a muscle to acknowledge our presence.

We stood in the foyer. Goldsmith descended the stairs. His height surprised me. Six-foot-four, maybe? Large, black-rimmed glasses covered a bronze-tanned face with deep-set, dark eyes. His curly, black hair looked more like a little rug atop his head.

Maybe a hairpiece?

He descended the stairs, studying the sheriff on his way down. "What's this about, officer?"

Butch Turnbull could not be intimidated by any man. A woman, yes. Maybe that's why he'd never married.

"I'm Sheriff Turnbull. With your permission, we'd like to check your typewriters. If you require a search warrant, we'll come back with one, but meantime we're gonna station some men around the house. Don't want any typewriters to go missin', now do we?"

Goldsmith squeezed the handrail till his knuckles turned white. Letting go, he quickly switched on his Hollywood charm. "Sheriff Turnbull, I'm Al Goldsmith. Pleasure to meet you." He didn't offer a handshake, only a hand wave in the air. "Go ahead, search *all* our typewriters. I believe we have two." He turned to O'Brien. "Banner, why don't you show the sheriff our typewriters?"

As O'Brien motioned for us to follow him, I glanced into the library again. Tully Ivey was in the wingback, her back to me. Smoke billowed from an ashtray. She turned a card and stared at it, then lit a cigarette.

Butch tugged on my shoulder. "Let's go." He then told Creel and Washington to check the entire house for any other typewriters.

The sheriff, Cox, and I followed O'Brien upstairs.

Finding a typewriter in one of the rooms, the sheriff told Cox, "Put some paper in and type the letter c."

Cox rolled a sheet and typed c several times. It was perfect. No flaw.

O'Brien leaned in for a closer look. "Why are you typing a c?"

"It doesn't concern you," Turnbull said. "Where's the other typewriter?"

O'Brien led us down a hallway, as he told Cox to join the others. "Make sure there aren't any other typewriters."

After Butch, O'Brien, and I entered the second room, O'Brien pointed to a typewriter in the corner on a small desk by the window. Then he left the room. Butch and I were too focused on the typewriter to notice O'Brien's departure. Butch sat and rolled in some paper. He pecked c across the page. No flaws.

"What's going on? He must've tricked us," Butch said. He spun around in the chair and stood. "Let's go."

We headed downstairs to wait on the other deputies to report. Goldsmith was waiting for us to descend the stairs. His eyes had narrowed, wrinkles stretched across his forehead. He stared at the big sheriff as he descended. They met, face to face—Butch on the last step, Goldsmith at the bottom of the stairs.

"Sheriff, if you ever want to set foot here again, you'll need to get a warrant. Now, get off the property."

"I'm not finished. My men are still checking the house. You said—"

"I changed my mind. I'm not asking. I'm telling you to leave. Right now." He pointed at the door. "Go get a warrant. Even a simpleton like you can understand what a warrant means."

The sheriff's jaw tightened. He yelled for his deputies to return to the foyer. Again, I glanced into the library. Tully Ivey and O'Brien were standing. She picked up a stack of papers and sat in the wingback. No doubt O'Brien had told her and Goldsmith about us testing cs on the typewriters.

Outside, Butch hitched up his pants. "He's the most arrogant jerk I've ever met. I'm not finished with him. Did you boys check the entire house?"

"No sir," Creel said. "We never finished before you called us."

Butch turned to Cox. "Get that warrant. Get the paperwork started today."

Not uttering a word in the car, the sheriff drove lightsouts—siren on—and dropped me off before he headed up to Greenlee.

A thought occurred to me later that afternoon when I was at the *Gazette*. South Mississippi has plenty of City National branches.

I called a few Gulf Coast bank branches.

"Ma'am, we don't have a deposit box with number 4918. We only go up to 1100 or so."

After two more dead-end calls, I had my newspaper intern call every City National branch in South Mississippi. It might take a few days, but it needed to be done.

And I needed to talk with Tully Ivey. Alone. I knew Butch would never approve it, so I took a chance.

I called the Grater house. Randy Carr answered. "Who's calling?"

I used a deeper voice. "Tell her a newspaper reporter would like to do a feature on her."

When I arrived, Randy Carr opened the front door. "That was you that called, wasn't it? You can't be here. You don't have a warrant."

"Mr. Carr, I think she'd like to tell me her side of the story—woman to woman—and get this whole mess cleared up. The sheriff and Mr. Goldsmith may not like each other, but I believe she trusts me. She'll be willing to talk. Go ask her."

Five minutes later, Tully Ivey and I were sitting in the library. Me? I was surprised she had agreed to meet.

"You realize I wouldn't be meeting with you if Alston were here," she said. "He wouldn't like it; but I have nothing to hide."

"I know you don't. I figured you'd like to set this whole mess straight."

"That's why I agreed to meet, darlin'. To end this sordid investigation."

I handed her a copy of the Dawkins note. "But I'm curious about something. When you first saw this note you never mentioned anything about Andrew Dawkins saying he loved you. Why is that?"

"While you may think you're very perceptive, Deputy, the answer is quite simple. I was thrilled to know there was proof of my innocence in some murder I had nothing to do with.

You need to understand that the tabloids have been hounding me about it for three years. If it weren't for Alston Goldsmith, I might not be making movies. He believed in me."

"Yet, you also stated you hardly knew Andrew Dawkins. In his note he says he loves you. Is that why you were down on the ground crying next to him?"

"Darlin,' I'll tell you what I told the sheriff—I love all the men." She released a steady stream of smoke. "I'll never forget my first movie opposite Cary Grant. Now he was a good-looking man. Ohh, but what yellow teeth. It was the cigarettes. He was too much of a man to use one of these," she said, raising her cigarette holder. "He preferred non-filtered."

Nothing I said or asked seemed to faze her. Trying to keep a straight face, I took shorthand of everything.

"The lockbox mentioned in the note," I said, "what do you know about it?"

"Why nothing, sugar. I do hope you find it, though, because Andrew somehow knows I was innocent in that terrible Rod Russell shooting." She tamped out her cigarette. "Now, is there anything else you need from me, darlin'? 'Cause I have more work to do on this script. I have to practice my Southern accent."

She waved the script in the air, and with it, waved me to the front door. "Randall, be a dear and show Mrs.—pardon me—Deputy McRae out."

What arrogance. I never wanted to interview her again.

Driving into Solo, I felt a strong urge to find out more about Rod Russell and Tully Ivey's connection. Maybe there was something there—maybe it would shed some light on Andrew's shooting. The only way to know was do some research in Los Angeles.

At home, I called American Travel in Memphis. The lady gave me the flight schedules. The best one departed Memphis, Thursday afternoon, one-fifteen.

"Perfect," I said. "How much is the ticket?"

"One hundred and forty-nine dollars."

Expensive, but I didn't hesitate. "I'll come by your office and pick it up."

No way would I tell Butch about this trip. He'd never approve. Besides, I was paying my own way.

8
City of Angels

I'd never seen palm trees. Tall ones, fat ones, on every street. And the cars!

"Over two million people live in L.A.," the taxi driver told me. I tried to imagine what two million people all bunched together would look like.

Heck, the Los Angeles library was as big as Solo.

With some help, I found the newspaper microfiche section and settled in. There were articles after articles about Tully Ivey. I learned she gave away hundreds of thousands to orphanages in Los Angeles and Minnesota.

No doubt she had some good qualities. So many orphanages. Maybe she was an orphan.

The tabloids, not the mainline newspapers, printed the most scuttlebutt. They had a heyday keeping up with her glamorous fund-raisers and her prolific public trysts with famous leading actors, the former owner of RTO Studios, even the President of The United States. If not for the invention of the long-lens camera, the public wouldn't have believed this stuff. Sure enough, several of the articles were about a young actor she'd been seeing. Rod Russell. Photos and stories of them together on boats, in the streets, at parties—all over. Then I came across a story about his death.

The reporter referred to it as a professional hit. Two gunmen walked into Morgan's restaurant one night and emptied their weapons on Russell. The photographs were gruesome. His lifeless body lay spread-eagle on a black and white tile floor. Blood was everywhere. The article claimed he was involved with the mafia. According to one source, "Russell had a reputation for big-time gambling."

Maybe he'd borrowed money and couldn't pay it back.

I made a copy of the article and continued searching.

Then this story appeared on the microfiche screen.

THE LOS ANGELES POST

THE LOS ANGELES POST • THURSDAY, MARCH 5, 1959

TULLY IVEY ACQUITTED

Tully Ivey, dubbed by Hollywood tabloids as "The Fair Slayer," left the Stanley Mosk Courthouse yesterday after the jury acquitted her in the Rod Russell murder trial. Russell had been convicted of assault and battery against the star in July of 1958.

The story continued in the same vein. This Russell character must've been a real dirt bag.

After an hour of searching the tabloids, I stumbled upon an obscure, but interesting article. This one from *The Hollywood Appeal*, May, 1959, implying Ivey may have paid the mafia to murder Russell.

...Some suspicion still hangs over the verdict. As one witness claims, the glamorous actress was seen arguing with Russell at Morgan's Restaurant on a previous night. The anonymous witness told this reporter she heard the word 'blackmail' used more than once during their dinner. Mrs. Ivey and Rod Russell are both reputed to have connections with Giamano Pileggi, head of the West Coast mafia, as well as the East Coast Kennedy family.

There was more to the story, but this was enough to get me thinking. I even came across a photo of Ivey seated next to Giamono Pileggi at Romano's Italian restaurant. He, a stocky, dark-complexioned man in a dapper three-piece suit; she, in a lowcut designer dress, blowing a smoke ring at the photographer. The photograph included so many people it wasn't suitable for publication. But, I did make a copy for later.

I knew for sure she was "connected." I found no other stories about Ivey and Rod Russell. The news of her escapades had stopped.

After searching through months of issues, the stories picked up again, out of the blue, from a reporter with *The Hollywood Appeal*. His articles included more than I'd seen in the mainline newpapers—he had found a second-hand witness to the Russell murder.

I used the library's pay phone to call the reporter. He had no problem giving me the name and address of his source—Joanna Whitfield. I hailed a taxi and paid a visit to her home in West Hollywood.

Stopping outside a small cottage-style house, I told the driver I might be there a while.

Joanna Whitfield answered the door and I introduced myself. She allowed me into her modest living room. Red Naugahyde furniture filled the space, along with a glass coffee table and an hourglass-shaped lamp bubbling up orange-colored goo. Strange.

After I explained the purpose of my visit, she seemed grateful I'd come, which surprised me. She made coffee and we sat in the living room.

"I told the police what I knew," she said. "But they didn't wanna hear it."

I grabbed my pen and pocket notebook. "What did you know?"

She talked and I wrote. After she finished, I had five pages of shorthand.

Joanna Whitfield, looking like a struggling addict of some kind, claimed Tully Ivey and Rod Russell had been arguing at Morgan's the week before the shooting.

Even more incriminating, she said Tully Ivey was at Morgan's the night Russell was murdered in cold blood. Joanna's brother was a police officer on the scene. He told her the restaurant manager recognized Ivey at the table with Russell—a detail the *Los Angeles Times*, the AP, United, all of them failed to mention. According to Joanna's brother, Ivey had excused herself to the ladies' room just before the shooters arrived. While she disappeared through a back door, the gunmen shot Russell in cold blood.

"Joanna, why do you think nobody, including the Los Angeles DA, picked up on this?"

"What do you think, lady? The studio! This is Hollywood, dear. There's no way they'd let their star get caught up in this mess. Not even the police commissioner wanted to hear what my brother had to say. The Hollywood tabloids were the only ones who kept writing about it."

She fluffed out her bleach-blonde hair and tilted her chin up. "I used to be an actress myself you know. Even dated Robert Mitchum. You know who he is?"

I wanted her to like me, so I played along with her nostalgic fantasy. "Of course I know who he is. What's he like in real life?"

"Oh, sweet, but a real wild man. He dropped me for some other actress, though."

"Tully Ivey?"

"No. It was Lila Leeds."

"What about your brother, the police officer? Where's he?"

Her face wrinkled into a bitter frown. “Two months after the Russell shooting, he was killed in the line of duty. ’Least that’s how the bogus report reads.” She reached for her coffee cup.

“I’m sorry about your brother. What about the restaurant manager who recognized Tully Ivey?”

“Missing. Nobody knows where she is. It’s Hollywood, dear.”

After an hour of scribbling notes, it was time to leave.

“I’ve taken up so much of your time, Joanna. I’m very grateful. Thank you for everything. You’ve been very helpful.” I shoved my pen and notebook back in my purse and stood. “May I have your phone number in case I need to reach you?”

“Sure,” she said, writing it on a piece of paper.

“Would you mind calling a taxi for me? I don’t know the number.”

Reaching for the phone, she glanced out the window. “I believe there’s a taxi outside waiting on you.”

“Oh, good. I didn’t think he’d hang around.”

I opened the door and waved to the driver, letting him know I’d be right out. She handed me her number, we shook hands, and I walked to the taxi, then waved to her as I slid in the back seat.

I was more convinced than ever Tully Ivey had something to do with Rod Russell’s murder. But how did it tie into Andrew Dawkins’s shooting? I would take this news to the sheriff—maybe even write a story in the Gazette.

“Thank you for waiting,” I said to the taxi driver.

"My pleasure."

His voice was deep, unlike the driver who'd brought me. As he sped off, he twirled around and said, "If you jump I'll turn around and run over you."

What the…? My heart slammed into my chest. "Stop this instant!"

It was too late. We were already swerving wildly through the neighborhoods. He waved a pistol in my face.

"Just stay calm, I'll get you there soon."

"Where?" An acute adrenaline rush overwhelmed me. "Where are you taking me? I want to go to the airport. Right now!"

"I'm afraid not, Mrs. McRae. I have orders."

How did he know my name?

He glanced at me and laughed. My mind was in overdrive, horrified even more by his tatoos and gold teeth.

"Hold on tight now," he said, laughing louder.

He skidded through every turn and every curve, narrowly missing cars, tossing me from one side of the taxi to the other. We quickly came to the freeway, where he zoomed in and out of traffic. My heart was pounding.

I needed to breathe into a bag.

My purse! I cupped the leather bag around my mouth and breathed heavily, in and out. I was in sheer panic mode when I remembered the six-inch hatpin. I dug it out and gripped it tight in my right hand. What choice did I have? I jammed it into his neck.

Blood spurted. I must've hit an artery.

He screamed. But not as loud as I did when we hit the barricade, careened off, and ran head-on into a light pole. Smoke billowed from the crushed hood.

I was already pressed against the back of the front seat before we crashed. That's what saved me. Or it could've been an angel. The impact hurt me less than the driver. The steering wheel was jammed against his chest.

My hand was covered in blood. His blood. He looked dead, so I crawled over the front seat and fell out of the passenger side door into the orange dust, scrub, and rocks. I must have crawled twenty yards farther. The car caught fire.

An ambulance took me to a hospital. Doctors poked me, and the lab techs took lots of X-Rays. A white jacket entered my room and announced, "No broken bones."

Good. Then something in a needle put me to sleep.

When I woke from the narcotics, my legs stung—scratches from the car crash. My ribs were sore. A bandage was taped to my left temple. I must've hit the driver's seat with my face. All believers have guardian angels. Mine had saved my life.

Two policemen strolled into my hospital room. One was over-weight, the other skinny as a rail.

They were impressed a deputy had come all the way to California to question a witness. When I mentioned Tully Ivey's name, they lit up.

"I remember reading about that in the papers," Skinny said.

"Some B-rated actor named Russell, He was murdered by the mob."

"I'm talking about a different shooting. Tully Ivey shot a man in Mississippi. You're thinking of the Los Angeles Rod Russell murder. Which you've never solved, by the way."

I caughed and the pain was worse.

"We didn't work the Russell case," Lumpy said with a defensive tone.

They questioned me for an hour. I told them everything—why I'd come to Los Angeles, all of it.

Then I remembered. "My purse! I had a large purse with important papers—"

"It's right here, Deputy," Lumpy said, placing it on my bed. "Looks like a bunch of newspaper articles and a notepad where you interviewed somebody. It's in shorthand. Can you tell us what it says?"

I told them all about Joanna Whitfield, then added, "Officers, I feel sort of sick. Hand me that trashcan. Quick."

Afterwards, my ribs felt like somebody had hit me with a hammer.

"I should buzz a nurse," Skinny said.

"No-I'll-be-fine," I wheezed. "You might hand me a cold wash rag, though."

Lumpy held up my notes. "Mind if we take this back to the station and have somebody transcribe it for us? We need the information."

I draped the wet cloth over my good eye. "I don't mind. But you're gonna have to promise you'll return it tomorrow. It's official Bethel County evidence."

"Actually, Deputy McRae, it's now Los Angeles County's evidence. It's evidence taken in our county. But, yes, we'll make a copy and bring it by tomorrow."

"Good. And the driver? What happened to him?"

"Dead on the scene. We're running prints through our database tonight. Oh, and we called your sheriff in Bethel County to let him know about this."

"I really wish you hadn't done that." I slapped the wet cloth back over my face. "I'm probably in trouble now."

"You came out here on your own?"

"I did. He'll take my badge away."

I took the damp cloth off and looked at them with my good eye. "How upset was he?"

"Not at all, ma'am. He seemed sympathetic, worried about you. I think he realized you may have opened a door to some nasty stuff going on down there."

"That's a relief." I laughed at his nasty stuff comment, but shouldn't have. "Awww, it hurts to move."

"Get some rest. We'll be by tomorrow. I'm sure we'll have some more questions," Skinny said. "You're lucky to be alive."

"I don't believe in luck," I said.

I stayed overnight in the hospital "for observation," the doctor said. "No internal injuries. Just some bruised ribs."

They'd never believe all this back home. Placing a collect call to Oneeda, I told her everything, and asked her to book a flight for me to Memphis. She called back with news about a flight departing the next night. A "red-eye" she called it.

"Good, maybe my red eyes can get some sleep on the plane."

"You don't sound so good, Martha. You sure you're able to fly tomorrow?"

"I'm gettin' outta here no matter what they tell me."

Skinny and Lumpy dropped by at three the next afternoon.

"Big news, Deputy McRae. We ran the prints last night. Looks like the driver was a low-life thug."

"The mafia?"

"Not sure about any organized crime."

"Did he have a record?"

"He had a record, but no outstanding warrants."

"How did a common thug find me? Why would he want to kidnap me?"

"I guess the answer died with him. But we'll question our snitches, see what we can come up with. Honestly, we don't expect to find much, sorry to say."

Skinny said, "Listen, I'm sure you're a little fidgety about riding in another taxi, so we're going to give you a lift to the airport later tonight. Okay?"

"Thank you. Very nice of you."

"The hospital has released you, right?"

"Of course."

Early the next morning, I arrived in Memphis, stiff and sore, found my car in the lot, and drove home. Oneeda, Father Compañero, Mary, and little Michael all welcomed me with banners and balloons. It was a happy occasion.

Until the sheriff dropped by.

9
Snooping

"Martha, if you pull one more crazy stunt like that again, I'll have your badge. Understood?"

"Yessir, I understand."

"Now," he pulled his khaki trousers up, "you've obviously knocked down a hornet's nest. Somebody wants you to stop snooping around. What did you find out?"

I was stretched out on the sofa, not wanting to move. I pointed to my purse. "It's all in there."

He took the articles, sat down and started to read. Along the way, he cussed several times, but always added, "Sorry."

"Sheriff, Tully Ivey was somehow involved in the Russell murder," I said, barely able to speak. "And the Los Angeles mafia is behind it."

"I believe you," he said, not bothering to take his eyes from the articles and notes I took from Joanna Whitfield. "Tell me about her. Is she credible?"

"Who, Joanna Whitfield? Yes, very credible."

He ran a hand through his flattop. "Well, looks like I need to ask Mrs. Ivey some more questions. Be interesting to know how she got herself tangled up in this. If she had a hand in the Russell murder, it could cast a different light on the Dawkins case."

"I'm going with you. I can spot a lie if she's telling one." Wishful thinking on my part.

After pondering for a few seconds, he said, "When will you be up to riding out there?"

"Give me one day. I'll be ready tomorrow. My ribs are healing." It was a lie, but I wasn't about to let him interview her without me.

He made his way to the door, then turned.."Oh, by the way, the fingerprint analysis from the note came back. Of course Dawkins's prints were on it. But so were Tully Ivey's."

"Wait. You're sure it was hers?"

"We got three good partials. They match her California driver's license."

He left. And I was left to wonder how her prints got on the note—and what it meant.

When we arrived at the Grater place, Goldsmith met us with arms crossed over his chest and a cocked brow. "What are you doing here?"

"I need to speak with Tully Ivey," the sheriff said.

"They're out shooting a few scenes. I'm on my way there now." His voice became arrogant. "Why are you here?"

"When do you expect her back?"

"It depends, Sheriff. Now, take your hand off me."

As soon as I guessed they might fight like two roosters, I slipped off upstairs and searched every room for the typewriter. When I came to Goldsmith's room, I spotted one on his desk. I loaded in a sheet of paper and typed the letter c. There it was. The ç. I ripped the paper out, stuffed it in my purse, and hurried downstairs to deliver the news to Butch, but Goldsmith was having his say with the big man.

"... how many times have I told you, Sheriff? You - don't - have - a - warrant! So, no, you may not search the premises. I'm not hiding anything, you understand, I'm just sick and tired of dealing with local yahoos. I'm going to complain to the governor if you don't leave now, this second."

"C'mon, Martha. Let's go."

Outside, I tried to stop him. "Butch, wait."

"Save it for the station," he said, already at the car door.

As we drove off, he said, "I hate that man."

I pulled the sheet of paper out, and pushed it over his steering wheel.

"What's this?"

"It came from Goldsmith's typewriter. It has the same ç."

He looked down at it. "How did you get this?"

I told him about my upstairs visit.

Butch dropped it in my lap. "But wait. Why didn't we find it the first time?'

"I have no idea. Maybe it was somewhere else."

"Well, I'll be." He grinned from ear to ear. "We've got to get that warrant and get back out here as soon as possible. I'm going to nail this turkey, Martha. I'm going to nail him."

We drove a mile or so before he said, "Good work, Deputy."

I'd never felt so proud.

"Don't let it go to your head. I've still got an eye on you. Besides, you're on probation."

"Probation? For what?"

"For violatin' my rules. You're not supposed to question anybody unless I give you the assignment."

"Yessir. Got it. Now, we know Goldsmith typed the note."

"How do you know it was Goldsmith? Those typewriters probably get used by the whole bunch of 'em."

"Yeah, you're right. Still, the note was in Dawkins's hand. How'd it get there?"

He gave a shake of his head. "You are something else, Martha McRae, something else. No, I don't have a clue how the note wound up in his hand. Not yet."

The next day, Butch told me he wanted to talk with Tully Ivey again. About the key this time.

"Did you get a warrant?"

"Don't need a warrant to ask questions."

He told me to listen in on a second line. Tully Ivey herself answered the call.

"Yeees?" she cooed.

"This is Sheriff Turnbull. I need for you to come to the station." He was curt, but professional. I thought he might have lost his taste for her. About time.

"Why, Sheriff, whatever in the world for?"

"I just have a few more questions."

"Would you terribly mind coming out here? It would be so much more convenient for me if you'd make the little trip here."

"Goldsmith doesn't want me out there without a warrant. We'll have one soon, but I need to speak with you before I come out with an army of men. Do you understand?"

"Alston? Ohh, I can persuade Alston to do anything. It won't be a problem at all. Besides, he and the crew aren't here. I'm really very busy with this script." I could almost hear her pout. "Sheriff, you'll do this for me, won't you?"

Butch wasn't sure what to do. He had no warrant to enter the house. After seconds of dead silence, he said, "Okay. But I want you to meet me at the front door. You'll have to invite me inside. Understood?"

"Oh, yes, siiir. I'll be the one in the nightgown."

Click. She hung up.

Staring off into the distance, Butch slowly replaced his phone on the base.

"Butch, she's crazy as a loon. You should take deputies."

"No, we don't have a warrant. Better if I go alone."

"I'm going with you. You can't stop me. I'll take my car if—"

"Martha, the governor's office called," he said, interrupting. "They want me to—and I quote—'take it easy on Ivey.' It's all about public relations. They mentioned Mississippi's reputation in the movie industry and junk like that. This is not good."

"Let me help. Woman to woman. I can handle her. I know more about her now."

Butch was antsy, pulling on his belt, staring out the window. "Okay, okay."

Deputy Cox strutted into the office. "Sheriff, I heard you talking about going out to the Grater house to talk with her. I'd like to come along."

I was happy about the sheriff's answer. "Nope. Too many of us. Stay here. Keep working on the warrant."

Butch and I drove out to the Grater house.

The door opened. She was lounged against the door jam, one hand on her protruding pelvis. A posing starlet. It was almost eerie, like one of her movie posters. No nightgown, though. Just a pink robe tightly hugging her hips, flowing to her ankles.

"Sheriff, it's so good to be back from Los Angeles and see you again." Then she looked straight at me. "And you,

Deputy—d e p u t y … I'm so sorry, I forgot your name."

Butch jumped in, "You remember Deputy McRae, don't you? May we come in?"

"Of course, of course. Come in. Yeees, I remember. McRae. Martha, isn't it?"

"Yes." I followed her swishy derriere as we walked. Me, mentally comparing mine with her perfectly shaped one.

As we walked, she engaged the sheriff in conversation. "I want to thank you for the hall pass."

"Hall pass?"

"Yes, you let me go home for a few days, and I want to thank you for it."

Turnbull ignored her. "Is anyone else here?"

"No, just my agent, Randall. The others are out shooting some B-roll."

"B-roll?"

"Filming the countryside," she said, waving a dramatic hand.

We walked into the library. Randy Carr was seated on the sofa. The sheriff nodded in his direction, and we took a seat. The furniture was still covered in plastic, except for one chair—the wingback. She sat, crossed her legs, and held a cigarette holder to her lips, waiting for Randy Carr to light it, which he did. Those strange-looking cards were on her side table.

Butch leaned forward on the sofa, sweating, rubbing his forehead. He glanced at Carr and back to Tully Ivey.

"Miz Ivey …" He rubbed his hands together like a nervous captain before his queen. "I just have a few questions. Let's start with what Deputy McRae here discovered in Los Angeles."

"Los Angeles?" She raised her eyebrows at me. "My dear, why, I didn't know you'd been to my most favorite city in the world. You should've informed me you were coming. I was just there. We could have had lunch at the club and talked all day."

Right. She was probably the one who had sicced the thug on me.

Butch ignored her comment to me. "I'd like to ask you about Rod Russell."

"Rod Russell? Oh, of course. The poor young actor who was murdered by those awful people."

"Tell me your version of what happened."

She began weaving a tale so convoluted and contrived I had to jump in. "Mrs. Ivey, I'd like to use the powder room if you don't mind. I'm very sorry about this, but, well, you understand."

"Of course, dear. Do you know where it is?"

"Yes, thank you. Oh, is anybody else here? I don't want to surprise anyone." I smiled. "If you know what I mean."

"Just us." She smiled back, then took a short drag from her cigarette.

I left the room as the sheriff began asking more questions. Only I didn't go to the downstairs powder room. I slipped up the steps. I could hear them talking downstairs as I walked into

Goldsmith's room. I looked for the typewriter.

It was gone.

Checking another room, I found the second typewriter, typed c a few times. No flaw. I then eased back downstairs as the sheriff was asking Ivey, "So you were at home when tis fellow, Rod Russell, was murdered?"

"Of course, my dear. As I've told everyone, I was home watching a new television show." She drew deeply on her cigarette holder, and blew out a smoke ring.

"Right," Turnbull said.

She shifted her attention to me. "Deputy McRae, did you find what you were looking for?"

"Yes, I did, thank you."

"Sheriff, do you have any more questions? If not, I'd like to get back to my script."

"No more questions for now. Thank you for your time."

As we were about to leave, she flipped a card from the deck and held it up for us to see.

"Ah, the High Priestess. Interesting."

The card was alluring and beautiful—a woman seated on some sort of cube surrounded by two columns, with trees in the background. I couldn't see many details, but it was mystical and full of imagery.

She looked at me. "Someday I'll tell you what it means for you."

I ignored her comment.

We said our goodbyes and left the property.

About to explode with the bad news as we drove away, I said, "Butch, I didn't go to the powder room. I went to the second floor rooms. I wanted to make sure the typewriter was still there."

"Goldsmith's typewriter?"

I nodded. "It's gone."

He cursed. "There has to be an explanation."

"Yeah, there is. Goldsmith threw it away so we couldn't find it. I think he figured we were on to him."

"You could be right." He tugged on an earlobe. "By the way, what's the deal with that card? That High Priestess stuff?"

"I saw those two weeks ago. They're tarot cards. Some people believe they can predict the future."

"Okay, so what's this High Priestess about?"

"I don't know. I'm gonna find out, though."

After supper, I broke my own rule. I had more than two glasses of sherry.

Mary, Father Compañero, and I sat in the parlor. I asked him, "How much do you know about tarot cards?"

"I know a little, from my youth in Mexico."

Mary chimed in. “I know a lot. You know… from my former life and all.”

“What are they for?”

“Some people believe the cards can predict the future,” she said. “There’s a different meaning for each one.”

“What does the High Priestess card mean?”

Mary’s eyes widened. “She turned the High Priestess card? Are you sure?”

“Of course I’m sure. Why? What’s it mean?”

She tapped her lips with a finger. “It means different things depending on the question, or as tarot readers say, ‘the search.’ Like the search for life’s meaning or guidancee for someone. It can relate to work, love life, or spirituality. Of course, it’s all bunk.”

“It’s satanic,” Father Paul said. “God forbids witchcraft.”

“I know. But it means something to *Tully Ivey*,” I said, eager to know more.

“If memory serves me correctly, the High Priestess indicates to her that you’re about to have a change in your work life,” Mary said. “The High Priestess card is particularly good for poets and writers. She probably thinks your intuitive powers are increasing and you may be inspired to be creative in your work.”

“Mary, that means nothing to me. It all sounds like mumbo-jumbo. And how’d you know all that?”

"Years of practice, honey, years on the street. Thank the Lord those days are over."

I didn't know what to say. Mary's story about the card only added confusion.

Later that night, I probably drank more sherry than I should have. I began to wonder about Tully Ivey. Should I feel sorry for her? Maybe she's just so insecure she uses tarot cards for guidance.

10
The Warrant

The next day, I felt sluggish, but went to the sheriff's office to write the report about my ç discovery. By the time I finished, Deputy Cox strolled in and headed to Butch's office, with me not far behind.

"Got the warrant. Just picked it up," Cox said. "What's next?"

"Get Creel, Washington, and Herring. We'll take three cars. I want a show of force when we get there. Baxter can hold the fort down till we get back. The typewriter's gotta be in the house somewhere. Are you feeling up to this, Martha?"

"I'd go if I was half dead."

Which was how I felt.

Speeding out to the Grater house with sirens blaring was a thrill, headache or not.

Butch switched off the siren when we pulled into the long white rock drive leading up to the house.

As our three squad cars stopped at the house, the front door opened. Six of us deputies met Randy Carr at the front door. "Goodness, Sheriff, you must be expecting some sort of army action here."

"Nope, son, we're just gonna make sure nothing leaves the premises. Now get in there and tell Golds—"

As if on cue, Goldsmith stepped outside and glared at Butch. "I assume you have a warrant, Sheriff."

"Right here." Turnbull handed it to him, then addressed his team. "Washington, take the back of the house. Nobody leaves. Herring, you watch from here. Cox and Creel, y'all come with me. You, too, McRae."

We walked around Goldsmith as he stood his ground, turning only his head to watch us strut through the front entrance.

We went straight up to Goldsmith's room. I was behind he sheriff, hoping to step in and see the typewriter back in its place. It wasn't there.

"Check the other rooms," Turnbull told the deputies. "Get all the typewriters."

Butch and I returned downstairs. Goldsmith and Carr stood in the foyer, looking up as we descended the long staircase. I stood behind Butch.

"Find what you're looking for, Sheriff?" Goldsmith said with an oily smile.

"Where is it?" Turnbull demanded.

"Where's what?"

"The typewriter. Your typewriter, Mr. Goldsmith. Where is it?"

"Sorry to disappoint you, but I don't own one." His eyebrows squished together with fake concern. "To be truthful,

I own several, in a manner of speaking. I'm the producer, remember? I pay for everything. But no, I don't personally own one. It looks as if you're chasing the wrong rabbit. Or should I say, the wrong typewriter?"

"We'll see. My men are searching the entire house. They'll find it."

"May I ask you a question?"

With no response, Butch hitched up his pants.

Goldsmith continued, "What is so important about this typewriter you're searching for?"

Again, no response from the sheriff; he simply walked around him.

Goldsmith turned to me. "You. You know what this is about, don't you?"

"Mr. Goldsmith, I don't offer information. You're the one who needs to offer information."

Side-stepping him, I joined Butch and the others in the back hallway. With a typewriter tucked under each arm, Creel said, "Found these two, Sheriff. Probably the same ones we found before. Whadda you wanna do with 'em?"

Butch looked around for a door, saw one, and led us all into a laundry room. "Find some paper," he said. "One of 'em has gotta have the faulty ç."

Creel left to find paper. He returned, rolled in a sheet, and typed c several times on one of the typewriters. Then, he went through the same procedure on the other typewriter. No ç on either one.

Creel raised his eyebrows. "What now, Boss?".

"Bring 'em with us," Butch said. "He tricked us again somehow. But the trick's gonna be on him. If he plans on writing any more movie scripts, he'll have to bring out the real one. These are going with us."

On the way out, I stopped and looked Carr in the eye. "Where's Tully Ivey?"

"If you must know, she's back in Los Angeles."

Goldsmith followed us outside. "You can't take my typewriters. What are you doing?"

"Evidence, Mr. Goldsmith, evidence," Butch said. "You'll get'em back after this is all wrapped up."

Goldsmith folded his arms across his chest. "You don't believe she shot him in self-defense, do you?" He pointed his finger at the Sheriff and shouted, "What do you people down here think you're doing? This is the most screwed up police business I've ever seen."

We took the typewriters and left dust hanging in Goldsmith's face. He was shouting something about the governor.

11
The Rector

One afternoon, a week later, I was in the kitchen chopping vegetables when Mary came home from her secretarial job at Calvary.

"Martha, I probably shouldn't be telling you this, but there's something you should know, now that you're a deputy and all."

I placed my knife on the counter and waited to hear this.

"She was in with Father Paul today. For over an hour.

"Who, Tully Ivey?"

"Yes."

"That's crazy. I thought she was in Los Angeles."

"I guess she's back. I just thought it'd be important for you to know."

"It is. Thank you."

After supper, Mary and Michael went to their back bungalow, while Father Paul and I enjoyed some pecan pie in the kitchen.

I figured the conversation would be touchy. "Father, may I ask a sensitive question?"

"Of course."

"Can you tell me why Tully Ivey was in your office?"

"Ahh, I should have known Mary would confide in you. But you have indeed raised a sensitive question, Martha. Very sensitive. You know I can't divulge a conversation between confessor and priest."

"But you're not Catholic. The secrecy between a confessor and priest is only in the Catholic Church. You're not Catholic."

"No, but I was brought up by Catholic aunts and uncles."

"Brought up? I don't understand."

He wiped his mouth and folded his napkin, placing it neatly on the table. "My parents never attended church. But my cousins were Catholic. I would hear them talk about the traditions around our dinner table. Maratha, some aspects of our life are part of our upbringing." His eyes pleaded with me to understand.

I didn't. "We're talking about a mixed-up woman who shot someone, and we still don't have all the details. I'm sure you understand the severity of the situation as much as you do the sensitivity of it."

"I'll tell you this much—she is a disturbed woman. A woman without meaning in her life. Yes, I have counseled her. Once. To help her move to a better place. But it's not something I wish to discuss. I hope you understand."

"Actually, I don't. We're talking about *evidence* here. You're not Catholic. You're a Protestant minister. Paul, for goodness sake, I need to know what she told you." I crossed my arms. "Besides, she's crafty. She's probably playing you."

"No, I believe she's sincere about getting help. I'd rather not talk about it."

I let my arms drop. I was getting nowhere with the rector.

"Tell me this. Why do you feel compelled to hold on to the confessor's secrecy? I'm involved in a serious situation. I'm simply asking you to be an Episcopal priest."

"Martha, you are undoubtedly the most persistent person I know." He cupped his hands together and sighed. "Okay, I'll tell you this much. She grew up in a Minnesota orphanage. Catholic. Very strict. One of the priests evidently dolled her up for beauty contests when she was young. Like ten or eleven. I suppose she was a beautiful little girl, even then. She was his special pet. He abused her. She ran away at seventeen, determined to make it in Hollywood—'whatever it took,' she told me."

I was beginning to feel sorry for her.

"And I'll add this," he said. "She used to attend confession on a regular basis. I believe she misses it." He paused. "Now, there's nothing else about her that could help you solve a murder. Will you trust me on that?"

"Of course."

I felt a strong urge to ask about his personal upbringing. I shouldn't ask. I really shouldn't. But I did anyway.

"Father Paul, you said you didn't grow up in a church-going family. May I ask how you became a Christian?"

He hesitated, and took a deep breath. "I've told very few people this story." He placed his cup on the table and looked me in the eye. "I was a teenager in Mexico, walking alone from Monterrey to Santiago, mad at God for this polio."

He reached down and rubbed the metal of his leg brace. "It was burning hot. All I could think about was the heat, the dust, and this polio. I complained the whole way. Then—in a flash—a swirl of sand, like a small tornado, formed in front of me; only, it was bright, like the sun. I heard a voice. At first, I thought it was the sound of the swirling sand. I'll never forget it." He paused.

"You heard a voice speak to you?"

He clamped his hands together in front of me. "I wasn't sure if the voice was audible or just in my head."

"What did it say?"

"It said, 'Paul, Paul, my grace is sufficient for you, for my power is made perfect in weakness.'"

"I've never heard such a story, except in the Bible. But what did the voice mean by 'made perfect in weakness?'"

A crease formed in his forehead. "I, too, was confused," he said. "I arrived in Santiago and told my uncle about it. He was amazed. He grabbed his Bible and read from 2 Corinthians.

Tú te has vuelto egoísta en la autocompasión. Dios quiere estés agradecido con lo que tienes. '"

I smiled. "You'll need to translate."

"He told me God had allowed Satan to harass me. He was speaking of my polio. He said I had become selfish in self-pity. God wants me to be grateful for what I have. He said God's grace is all I need."

"Your uncle gave you quite a sermon."

"No, God did."

"Is that when you decided to become a rector?"

"That came much later." He retrieved his coffee cup. "Now, Martha, I've told you more than I should about Tully Ivey. So, it's your turn to tell me what you plan to do with this information."

"I sort of feel sorry for her. But I'd like to get her alone. Get her out of that Hollywood mindset. I'd like to know what makes her tick."

"I wouldn't do that if I were you."

"Really? Why?"

"She could twist your mind into something you'd regret."

"Oh, I doubt that."

"Are you sure?" He placed his cup on the table and stood. "I hope you're right. Forgive me, but I must go and rewrite my sermon."

"Rewrite it?"

"Our discussion has also been fruitful for me. I'm going to change the sermon to *God's Sufficient Grace*."

He limped up the stairs as I donned my apron to clean the kitchen.

12
Extras

Thirty minutes later, the phone rang.

"Deputy McRae, this is Banner O'Brien. I hope I haven't called too late."

"No, it's fine. How can I help?"

"Mr. Goldsmith wanted me to call and let you know we're about to resume filming, and we don't have enough extras. He'd like to invite you to be in the movie."

"Oh, really? That's a surprise."

"Do you know what an extra is?"

"It's somebody who's in a movie but doesn't have a speaking part, right?"

"Exactly. You'd be in the background, like part of a crowd. Only in this scene we'll be shooting some close-ups."

I might learn something. "Yes, I'd like to see how it's done. Will you be directing it?"

"Yes ma'am. I will."

"Where should I go? What else do I need to know?"

"We'd like for you to wear a blue dress. We'll be shooting at Parchman Penitentiary."

I almost choked. "Young man, are you aware of my history with Parchman? How does Mr. Goldsmith know I witnessed Sartain's execution?"

He was silent.

"What's this about?" I demanded.

"Mrs. McRae, it's a chance to be in a movie. And it pays money."

"No, I mean what's the scene about?"

"Oh, the scene. Well, it's a realistic shot of the execution chamber."

"Ahh, perfect, just what I was afraid of. The execution of Sonny Sartain, right?"

"I'm just doing what Mr. Goldsmith asked."

I needed to regain my composure and think it through.

"Who else from Solo will be there?"

"I don't have the list in front of me, but I'm sure you'll know plenty of them."

"Let me think about it and call you back."

Oneeda walked in shortly after I hung up.

I faced her with my fist propped on my hip. "You won't believe what just happened. Al Goldsmith wants me to be an extra while they shoot a scene about Sartain's execution."

Still smacking on her gum, she did her best to strike a Hollywood pose. "I've always wanted to be in a movie. Can I go with you?"

"I'm not even sure I should go. I told them I'd think about it."

"Think about it? I'd die to be in a movie."

"Oneeda, remember my visit to Los Angeles? Somebody doesn't like me. What if it's Goldsmith?"

"Oh, you're right."

Still conflicted, I sat and pondered.

"What is it, Martha? What are you thinking?"

"I'm not sure. There're guards everywhere. I doubt anything could happen."

"You're going?"

"I'm not sure."

The next day, I called O'Brien. "When should I be there?"

"Thursday morning," he said. "Makeup starts at seven-thirty. If you arrive by seven, you'll be safe."

Be safe. That was difficult to ignore.

I arrived at Parchman precisely at seven on Thursday morning, dressed in blue. Prison guards covered the entire premises. Three large eighteen-wheel trailers and two fancy traveling coaches sat out front of the prison. One must've been the star's dressing room and the other for the producer and director. Or maybe Mario Mastrioni.

Prison guards covered the entire premises. Randy Carr was

waiting for me. After a curt hello, he escorted me through the main entrance building, outside to the yard, and then into another building. It was all too familiar and brought back memories of Sartain's execution.

He handed me a one-page *Extra's Release* form. "You'll need to sign this."

I read it. For the sum of $50, they would own all rights to my image in the movie. I would have no recourse for a lawsuit of any kind. Probably all typical, so I signed it.

"Time to go," he said.

We arrived in the prison library. Goldsmith was standing near the back wall, watching as the extras came in. Carr said, "This is where we're holding our pre-production meeting."

Goldsmith approached me. "Ahhh, Mrs.—please, pardon me—*Deputy* McRae, I meant to say. Glad you could participate in our scene today. Randy, why don't you take the deputy and the others to makeup." He never offered his hand, and neither did I. Before he left, he addressed the others in the room. "Thank you, and I'll see all of you later." He turned to leave.

What a strange man. He comes across as a rude bully at the Grater house. Today he's professional and sweet as sugarcane.

There were no fancy trailers for extras. We were all escorted to vacant prison cells. I recognized only a few of the extras.

Gloria was my makeup artist. As she began working on my eyelashes, which hadn't seen mascara in months, I said, "Would you believe it if I told you I've spent time in one of these cells before?"

"Sweetie, what in the world would a nice lady like you be doing in a prison cell?"

I told her the whole story. Twenty minutes later, I looked at myself in the mirror. "I have to say, I don't believe I've ever looked so glamorous. Been a long time since I've had on makeup."

"Sweetie, my job is to make you look good on film."

Just then, I heard O'Brien barking orders from the main door to the cell block. "All stylists, wrap it up. I need extras on set in five minutes."

We marched to the building housing the gas chamber. The other extras were buzzing about how exciting this was going to be. Me? I was becoming more and more uneasy about it.

We were led into the witness room with the thick glass windows—the same room I'd sat in two years ago to witness Sonny Sartain's execution. Four rows of straight-back church chairs filled the room. The execution chamber was painted in light green, giving the room a sick, eerie look.

There were two guards in the rear of the witness room; but they looked more like actors. Taped on the back of each chair were our names. Mine was the same seat I'd sat in at Sartain's execution. I felt sick. None of this seemed right. Was I caught in a trap?

"Where's Superintendent Harris? I'd like to speak with Superintendent Harris. I know him and I—"

O'Brien strutted into the room and interrupted me. "Ladies and gentlemen, thank you for coming. I must say, we're happy with our selection of extras for this scene. We have two cameras in the room. I'm sure you've seen them. We'll be shooting without rehearsals today. We'll be filming your reactions. Very tight shots of your faces. Do not look into the camera lens." He pointed to the cameras. "I do not want you to 'act.' Do not *play* to the camera. Merely give me your real feelings as the action unfolds."

I thought of asking for the restroom and running away.

"If any of you want to get up and walk out," he said, "please do it after you hear me say 'that's a wrap.' The doors are now locked, but we'll open them as soon as the scene is finished. It should only take a few minutes. Does everyone understand?"

I looked around. Nobody's hand had gone up. But I raised mine.

"Deputy McRae, what is it you don't understand?" O'Brien was nice, but firm.

All of the extras looked at me like I was interfering with their moment of fame. I slowly lowered my hand.

"Good, then you understand," he said. "I'll be in the other room. My assistant will be here. He'll let you know when we're rolling film and when we stop action. Remember, be yourself. Don't try to act."

After he left the room, I raised my hand, looking at one of the guards behind me. "Could you tell me where the nearest restroom is, please?"

"I've been instructed to keep the doors locked, ma'am, until he finishes shooting this scene. I'm afraid it's too late to leave the room." He had no sympathy whatsoever for my fictitious bladder problem. "Now, if all of you would line up at the door, we'll start with shooting each of you taking your seat; and please, take the same seat you're in now. Okay, everybody to the door."

"Where is Superintendent Harris? I'd like to know." I was agitated and didn't care two hoots if I was disrupting their little make-believe scene. Before anyone could even answer me, a crewmember stepped in front of a camera, held up a slate, and clapped a black, wooden board. Written in chalk on the black slate was, *Scene 24, Take 1.* The photographers began moving their huge Panavision cameras around the room, aimed at us "witnesses" as we sat. The film roared as it went through the two circular camera reels. We sat and turned our attention to the chamber.

I became riveted on the actor being escorted into the airtight chamber. He looked like Sonny Sartain, scraggly hair and all. Two attendants strapped him into a chair. There was a black box under it.

Once they left the chamber, the room was sealed. An actor, playing the role of Superintendent Harris, gave a signal to the executioner. The black box released a steady stream of smoke. All fake, off course.

I had remembered everything about Sartain's demise. There was no black box. It was a pail of sulfuric acid underneath the chair. Above that was a canister of sodium cyanide. When the executioner gave his signal, the canister tipped over and mixed with the sulfuric acid. The concoction became hydrogen cyanide gas.

The white vapor seeped up beneath the actor's chair. He tugged and jerked on his wrist straps. Within seconds the room was filled with a thick white vapor. Unlike Sartain, who had sucked in the gas as quickly as possible, the actor held his breath, evidently trying to delay the inevitable.

Where Sartain had passed without a struggle, this actor followed Andy Chinn's script. He went into convulsions, slamming his head on the anchoring pipe behind his chair. His eyes bulged, about to pop out, his neck muscles strained, and his fists turned white at the knuckles. Finally, he sucked in enough of the poisonous air to release a primal scream.

This couldn't be! Sartain did not die like this. He had passed without a struggle. Seconds later, the actor's head fell over to one side.

I breathed a sigh of relief.

No sooner had I begun to relax than the actor's legs and feet began gyrating against the straps. His chest heaved upwards and fell back. His entire body went into convulsions. His head began thrashing out of control. Foam oozed from his open mouth.

I felt sick to my stomach. The camera moved in for close-ups on my face and two other extras. I was in shock. The rest of the witnesses dropped their heads into their hands, not looking any longer at the scene inside the chamber.

I jumped to my feet. "Stop this!"

The whir of the camera was on-going.

"Stop it," I yelled, staring through the viewing window. "This is *not* how it happened. He was not executed like this!"

Director O'Brien's voice came through the sound system, "Cut! That's a wrap. Good work, everybody. Got what we needed on the first take. Just fantastic. I love it."

Good work? "What a bald-faced lie," I said to the assistant director in the room. "That's not how it happened. Not even close. I was here."

"Ma'am, I think the director got what he wanted." He addressed the group as a whole. "Thank you all for being here. You may collect your money in the trailer outside the front entrance."

I marched toward him. "Sir, I'd like to see what you filmed."

"Sorry. Not part of your contract, lady."

"Do they intend to use all of it? What I said and all?"

"There was no sound equipment for this scene, ma'am."

I didn't even bother to pick up my check on the way out.

13
The Gazette

Two days later, Oneeda came bursting through my front door, yelling, "Martha, Martha, come out here! *The Gazette's* on fire."

I dropped my plate on the counter. It broke into pieces. I charged out of the house with Mary and Father Paul close behind. Two streets over, in the center of town, we saw the smoke. We ran as fast as we could.

A dozen people had gathered in front of the *Gazette*, dragging a water hose as close as possible to the side windows. The feeble stream from the hose was about as good as spit on a campfire.

I moaned, "Please, don't let my newspaper burn down."

A bucket brigade started from Kirk's Feed & Seed store. I joined in and passed buckets down the line to the brave men covering their faces as they dumped water through the smoking windows.

Soon, we had volunteers forming a solid line of help, the entire town eventually came out to help. Or watch. There was nothing most could do anyway. They might as well watch.

Someone yelled, "Did anyone call Parchman for their fire truck?"

A shout came back, "They're on the way."

Wiping sweat from my forehead, I looked up and recognized every face on the line and in the crowd. I was proud of my neighbors. My friends. My Solo.

From the corner of my eye, I spotted a lone figure outside Annie's butcher shop—a stranger.

The lady next to me set her bucket at my feet. "Get with it, Martha. Pay attention!"

Grabbing the next bucket from her, I glanced up toward the man again. He was gone.

The fire truck came barreling down Main Street, siren blowing, men hanging on the sides. We all clapped and whistled.

An hour later, the fire was extinguished. So many friends hugged me, saying how sorry they were. The crowd broke into groups to chat about the day's events.

I wouldn't trade Solo for anywhere. Friendship's true grit had been on display.

After most folks had gone home, the sheriff and the county fire marshal walked into my *Gazette* building.

After fifteen minutes or so, the sheriff yelled, "Martha, you can come in now."

Not sure if I was ready to see the devastation, I asked Mary and Oneeda to walk in with me. We covered our noses and mouths with handkerchiefs. They put their arms around me and we walked through the rubble together, through the front office, where the damage wasn't so terrible; to the back printing room, where the scene brought us all to a halt, mouths open, not able to speak. I wanted to cry.

Surely this was what hell smelled like. Black soot everywhere. The file cabinets—where I stored my old *Gazette* editions—were smoldering. My heart sank to my knees.

"Don't touch anything," Butch warned from the back corner of the room. He and the fire marshal were bent over, brushing a cloth across the floor.

Mary lowered her handkerchief and spoke first. "Martha, the front office doesn't look too bad. I don't know about this printing press, though. Will it work?"

"Martha," Butch yelled. "It started back here. Don't know what the ignition source was, though."

"Thank you." My voice was so timid he couldn't have heard my gratitude. I looked at Mary. "I'm sorry, you asked me something?"

"The printing press. Will it work?"

"I won't know until it's cleaned up."

Everything was covered in soot. And me, in self-pity.

Butch walked over. "Martha, it could've been worse if Parchman hadn't shown up."

"I suppose."

As he was leaving, I turned to Mary. "How will I ever… ?"

"We'll help you."

"We'll start tomorrow," Oneeda added.

I loved them both. "You're right, Oneeda. Tomorrow. Right now, I'm going home, put my feet up, and have a glass of sherry. Would y'all care to join me?"

We hugged.

At home, we did drink some sherry. Even managed to laugh about the bucket brigade chaos. Sometimes it helps to look tragedy in the face and laugh about it. Sometimes.

When Father Compañero came in, I became morose, but was determined not to cry about it anymore.

I looked him in the eye, and said, "How will I be able to write another story?"

He put an arm around me.

Dropping my head, I muttered, "I suppose it's God's doing. His will."

He took his arm away and looked straight into my eyes. "No, Martha, it's not God's doing. It's Satan's. God just allowed it."

"Why? Why would he allow it? There's truth to be told, and I'm not able to write about it now."

"Satan wants you to quit. But God never allows more hardship than we can handle. He wants to build our faith. Sometimes to test us."

I sat. I'd heard enough preaching. "I used to think I could handle anything Satan threw at me," I said. "But now, with this—

the fire, the taxi in Los Angeles—I'm thinking of dropping the whole thing." I slapped my legs. "Farewell to the *Gazette*. Just walk away from it all."

"Really? That's how you feel? I want you to think about something I learned in seminary. 'When we push through the unknown, things become clearer. If we don't keep pushing, the unknown becomes our enemy.'"

"How do I push through it?"

"You should start by asking God what he wants you to do. You should pray"

"Right now, I don't think I understand prayer."

"What do you mean?"

I shifted in my chair to face him fully. "If God is completely sovereign and knows what's going to happen beforehand—which you've told us many times—I've often wondered why I should even bother to pray. What's the point?"

"Because he said we *should* pray. He wants a relationship with us. How else could we have one if we don't talk to him?"

"That's it? That's the reason we should pray?"

"No, that's not all. He wants us to need him—to need his guidance, his protection, his wisdom. Besides, he answers the prayers of those whose will is in tune with his. God's answer is peace in our hearts. Satan's answer is fear." He gave me a sly smile. "And you'll never know what he wants you to do until you ask him."

"Then I guess I need to pray about it."

That night, I prayed for peace.

I had no idea the next phone call would be anything but peaceful.

PART II

Hollywood

"As for the rich in this present age,
charge them not to be haughty,
nor to set their hopes on the uncertainty
of riches, but on God, who richly
provides us with everything to enjoy."

— 1 Timothy 6:17

14

Who Knows?

"The fire was only a warning," the muffled voice on the phone said. "We don't want you writing about this Dawkins business. Next time, it'll be your home. With you in it. Understood?"

My voice shook, "Yes, I understand."

Click. The voice was gone.

I was scared. Not only for me, but for Mary, Michael, and Father Compañero.

I told Father Paul about the call. Mary was in Greenlee with little Michael.

"What would you do if you were me? Wouldn't you just drop this whole thing?"

"I think you should go to the sheriff," he said. "Tell him about the threat."

"I'll go, but I think he's star-struck. He's hardly approved of my involvement in this from the start."

Later, Oneeda dropped by. I told her about the phone call. She idly tapped her finger on the table, like she was thinking. "I remember a movie where gasoline was used to burn a house. The bad guys were trying to scare a private eye away from pursuing a case. Guess who stared in it? Tully Ivey."

"Really? That's interesting." I had regained some of my fortitude. "What's the name of it?"

"*The Lost Stranger.*"

"Can we get a copy of the script?"

"No idea," she said. "Maybe from the library. I can research it and find out. Want me to?"

"Yes, please. Maybe we can figure out who knew how to burn my Gazette down.""

She reported back two days later. No copies of the script were available from the Salem library. And the movie was out of circulation. "The Los Angeles library doesn't even have a copy. But I'm sure RTO Studio does," she added with a twinkle in her eye.

"So, how do we get a copy of it?"

"Leave it to me." She said, smacking on her Juicy Fruit.

Next morning, around eight, Sheriff Turnbull rang me. "It was arson all right. Gasoline. I'll have to report this to the DA and pursue it as a new case."

"There's something else, Butch. I don't think Tully Ivey had anything to do with it." I stretched the phone cord around the corner to a pot of water and turned the heat to high.

"Why do you say that?".

"Because I received a threatening phone call last night. I'm pretty sure it was a man. The voice was muffled, though. Said he'd burn my house down if I wrote anymore stories about the movie."

"It's gotten dangerous, Martha. Probably one of the movie crew. I'll investigate it."

"Look, Butch, don't worry about the *Gazette*—it'll just take your attention off the Dawkins case. Let me help you focus on that. This fire was an outright diversion to get us off track. You know it was."

"I'll investigate both. Don't concern yourself with my job."

We said our obligatory goodbyes and hung up. I dropped the spaghetti noodles in the boiling pot and watched them turn limp—sorta how I felt.

Next day, it was time again to visit Tully Ivey.

Her agent, Randy Carr, answered the door and escorted me in. I sat in the parlor while he fetched the queen.

Her entry was always the same—dressed in some elegant get-up, swishing her way into the parlor, dark red hair flowing like a Clairol model.

"Darlinnng, so good to see you," she said, breathing out the words like they'd come from Mae West in *Goin' To Town*. "Deputy… let's see, d e p u t y…"

“McRae,” I said, standing to greet her. She didn’t shake my hand. Typical.

“Oh, I am so sorry to hear about your little newspaper.” She sat in the wingback, slowly letting herself recline into the chair’s back, comfortable in her own skin. The tarot cards were on the table. She picked up a cigarette and waited for Carr to light it.

“No worries. I’ll have my paper up and running soon.” I sat back down. “But I’m not here on newspaper business. I’m here to ask you a few questions about the night of August tenth.”

“Why go right ahead, deputy. I have nothing to hide.” She tossed her head up, took a drag from the long-stemmed black holder, and blew smoke upwards in a steady gray stream.

“We can’t seem to locate the key, the one Andrew Dawkins left on the ledge.”

“Dear, if you can’t find it, I certainly can’t,” she said, laughing and looking over at Randy Carr.

Turning to me she said, “Darlin’, did y’all consider another aw-topsy?” She obviously was practicing her Southern accent; but her question was more intriguing.

“What would another autopsy tell us?”

She dropped the fake accent. “Deputy, did the coroner look in his mouth, or take a picture of his stomach?”

“I’m not following you.”

“My dear, what if he held the key in his mouth while he was about to tape the note on my window? Why can’t you people think? Think, darlinnng, think."

She was right. The corner should've at least searched Andrew's mouth. No way to take a picture. "We don't have an X-Ray machine in Solo."

She released another thin burst of burnt tobacco. "No surprise there," she said. "But that key could still be right in front of your nose—or his nose, for that matter."

His nose? That seemed sorta callous.

"Randall, be a dear and get me a vodka soda. And bring one for the Deputy."

"No thanks. I'm on duty. In fact, I have another question." I leaned forward. "There's the matter of the tape on the note. Tape was placed on the face of the note so it could be read by someone standing outside the window, not inside. What do you know about that?"

"I have no idea, darlin'."

Randy stood and acknowledged us both. "Excuse me for a minute."

After he departed, I asked her, "Would you mind if I have a look around?"

"Not at all. Do you think you're going to find some tape?"

"What if I do?"

"Go ahead, look all you want. But first, let me turn a card and see what's in store for you."

I stood while she dealt a card. It was an illustration of a sad person surrounded by five cups. "I'm so sorry. It's the Five of Cups," she said. "The card's meaning is quite simple—sadness, grief, disappointment, and regret await you."

"I don't think so," I said, and started my search.

I went to her bedroom first, where I caught a glimpse of Carr entering the powder room down the hall. I checked her bedroom and found no tape. I made a quick search of the drawers in each room and returned downstairs. No tape. Ivey and Carr were seated in the library, playing with the tarot cards.

As I walked in she dealt another card.

"Oh, dear," she said. "The Fool. Never let another person control your life. Live in the present and trust in your own abilities. This is the way of the Fool." She placed the card down and said, "It's my way."

"I don't believe in tarot cards. In fact, I find them evil." I sat on the sofa opposite her and clasped my knees, trying to look as steely-eyed as possible. "I have just one more question. What do you know about the governor's lockbox at City National Bank in Salem?" I hoped to catch her off guard, see if she flinched. But she didn't. Instead, she twisted the question into her own personal objective.

"You know, I would love to meet your governor. In fact, when I shoot on location, most governors invite me to a special state dinner. I have some fabulous designer dresses I adore wearing. You know what I mean."

I smiled. "I'm afraid not, Mrs. Ivey. I don't own any designer dresses."

"Randall, call the governor's office and find out why they haven't announced a party for me. And order one of my designer outfits for Deputy McRae—one of Harvey Simms's collections. She'll look good in it."

"That's very kind of you, Mrs. Ivey, but I—"

She glared at me with narrowed eyes. "Deputy McRae, please don't call me Mrs. Ivey again. Why don't you call me '*Miss Ivey*'?"

I was stunned by her arrogance.

She continued. "Now you say you haven't found the lockbox?"

"No, we haven't."

"Dear, how many banks around the country do you think have the name City National Bank? There must be thousands from here to California."

I froze. Didn't know what to say.

"Dear, you need to travel more often."

Carr piped up. "What do you people do all day at that police station?"

"You raise a good point, Mrs.—excuse me—ma'am."

"*Ma'am*? Now I like that. It's sooo Southern. I just love it. I've been practicing my Southern accent for this part, you know."

Carr said, "Looks like we've done your job for you, deputy. Why don't you run on back to the station and follow up on Miss

Ivey's suggestions?"

"I will. Those are some good ideas, I must admit. Thank you for your time."

I needed to drop this whole investigation business. I had no clue what I was doing.

"Deputy McRae," her voice held sympathy, "I like you. I don't want you to get the wrong impression about me. But I've seen most of these clues in my movies. I could practically be a detective."

"Thank you, ma'am. I believe you could."

I left for good.

Afterwards, I had a lot to think about. I was getting nowhere. Should I resign? Quit?

But something tapped my shoulder—think. She had wanted us to find the lockbox; it held the key to her innocence in the Rod Russell murder. And now she wanted to meet the governor. Maybe she'll try to convince him to stop the Dawkins investigation. I needed to get myself invited to that party.

15
The Interrogation

In the sheriff's office, I tossed out the idea of exhuming Andrew Dawkins's body, to determine if the key was in his mouth.

Deputies Cox, Creel, and Washington stood in the back of the room, snickering at my suggestion.

Turnbull stretched out over his desk toward me and said, "Martha, that's the most ridiculous idea I've heard since you talked me into hiding on the floor between the Calvary pews to hear Annie's confession."

I had to smile. But quickly got back on task. "Think, Butch, where else could the key be? It couldn't just vanish into thin air."

He tossed his hat on the table and scratched his head. "In his mouth you say? How's that possible?"

I gave him the same reasoning Tully Ivey gave me—to hold the key in his mouth while he taped the note on the window.

Butch scratched his head again, thought some more, and said, "I'll be darn, you could be right. Did you tell her about the tape on the note?"

"I did. And I searched every room. No tape. But, I didn't have time to search everywhere. Carr could've even taken it before I got to her bedroom."

Butch was buying in to the rationale. "She could be right about the key, though," he admitted. "I'll arrange for an exhumation. They'll do an X-Ray and re-bury him. I'll get a judge to okay it."

"There's more," I said. "She gave me an idea none of us considered. There are City National Banks all over the country. The note didn't mention any specific City National Bank."

Sheriff Turnbull blinked and blinked some more. He was processing all this information and likely wondering why he hadn't thought of these tips.

"Okay, okay," he said, "Dawkins probably put it in a Mississippi branch. I'll get a subpoena for the autopsy, and I'll get our men to start calling all the City Nationals in Mississippi."

"I've sorta already done that. Called 'em all—at least my assistant did. Anyway, there's only one deposit box with number 4918. The governor's."

"The gov-ern-or?" He plopped down in his swivel captain's chair. Leaning back against the wall, he expelled two lungs of hot September air.

"The gov-ern-or?" he said, again dragging the word out, shaking his head.

"We should ask ourselves if the governor could somehow be involved," I said.

"Not a chance. We won't be investigatin' the governor in something that's likely nothing more than a coincidence. You said it yourself, there are other City National Banks we need to contact."

"Butch, you know I don't believe in coincidences."

If my hunch was right, the governor would soon be throwing a party for Tully Ivey. How could I get an invite?

The next day I called for his chief of staff, Mr. Harland Rodgers.

The receptionist rang me through. I explained to Rodgers, "The actress, Tully Ivey, has been involved in a shooting up here, and I need to keep an eye on her at the party."

"Deputy, I already know about the shooting. What I don't understand is how you knew about any party. I just got word about it from the governor yesterday. I haven't even begun to make arrangements."

"Do you at least have a date, so I can put it in my calendar?"

"Hold on," he said. "Yes, here it is, November second."

"And the time?"

"We haven't settled on a time, but these honorary dinners usually start at six-thirty. Give me your full name and address and I'll make sure you receive an invitation."

I gave him my home address, not the sheriff's department. No way I wanted Butch to know I was attending the governor's private party for Tully Ivey.

Walking into the department office the next morning, I saw all the deputies and Turnbull gathered in the main room, most of them sitting on the sides of their desks, discussing Goldsmith's typewriter.

"It's got to be in the house, somewhere," Cox said.

"No it don't," Creel said. "He coulda ditched that typewriter and replaced it with another. Maybe it went back to California with Tully Ivey. Why can't we get some sort of warrant from Los Angeles and search his place out—"

"I've had it up to here with warrants," Butch barked, raising an arm above his head. He jerked his arm around and pointed towards the interrogation room, "I want to get Goldsmith inside that tank and show him how we handle arrogant jerks like him. I'll get him to confess. He ain't met his match yet."

Butch was still stewing over his encounter with Goldsmith. After deputies Cox and Creel left to retrieve Goldsmith, I remained quiet, at my desk, eager to witness the Sheriff's interrogation techniques through the one-way mirror.

Before the deputies returned with Goldsmith, Butch came out of his office. "Martha, when we were typing those c letters at the Grater house, do you think O'Brien told Goldsmith what we were doing?"

"I do. I remember O'Brien leaving the room when we were focused on the second typewriter. Then, when we came downstairs, he and Goldsmith were in the library. That's when Goldsmith told you to get a warrant. Remember?"

"Yes. You could be right. O'Brien told him we were typing cs. That's how Goldsmith knew to get rid of the typewriter."

Ten minutes later, Cox and Creel escorted a laughing Goldsmith through the back door of the department.

"Sheriff, I can't wait!" Goldsmith yelled. "I'm going to make a movie about your department—how absurd it is. And the whole state of Mississippi! The governor will get a kick out of it, don't you think?"

Turnbull spread his large hands around each hip. "You're the one who's gonna get a kick. You're coming with me."

I eased into the viewing room while Cox and Creel brought Goldsmith—still laughing—into the tank and placed him in a chair opposite Turnbull at a small metal table.

"Leave us," the sheriff said to his deputies.

Goldsmith smiled as they walked out. Then he frowned and faced Turnbull. "If you think for a New York second you'll have any influence over me whatsoever, I'll tell you—"

"Shut up. I want to know what you did with the typewriter. O'Brien told you what we were doing upstairs, didn't he?"

"I don't know what you're talking about. Am I under arrest? Because if I'm not, I need to get back to my movie production."

Turnbull launched his hefty body across the table so fast we almost missed it. He snatched Goldsmith's shirt and yanked him eyeball to eyeball. "You didn't answer my question. What – did – you – do – with – the - typewriter?"

Goldsmith knocked the sheriff's hands away and glared at him.

Butch caught a breath of air and settled back in his chair. "The typewriter. You took one of the typewriters from the Grater home, Mr. Goldsmith. It's what we call obstruction of justice in a murder trial."

"A murder trial! That is utterly preposterous." Goldsmith bellowed. "Don't tell me you're charging Tallulah Ivey for murder."

"That's exactly what I'm saying," Turnbull said, much calmer, leaning back in his chair.

It was the first time I'd heard Butch mention Tully Ivey's involvement in Andrew Dawkins's death. I about jumped out of my seat, elated he was showing some gumption.

"And before I bring her in, I want to know where the typewriter is. Do you understand me?"

"I have no clue where it is. One of the crew must've borrowed it. It could be back in L.A. for all I know." Goldsmith crossed his arms over his chest. "I know you're trying to do your job and all, but if you arrest Tully Ivey, several heads will roll. Trust me. It would shut down our filming again. And I promise you, the governor will not allow it. Did you know he's throwing a big soirée for Tully next month?"

"Good. Let 'em throw… whatever he wants for her. I don't care."

"Sheriff, unless you're going to arrest me for some crime I didn't commit, might I suggest you release me right this minute."

Butch hollered toward the two-way mirror. "Cox, Creel, take him back to the Grater house."

Butch was still fuming when they left.

"I'm glad you didn't arrest him," I said.

"Yeah, why?"

"We don't have enough evidence. Not yet."

"I know. I wanted to see if I could shake him up, get him to give up the typewriter. Now I'll probably have the governor raining hell down my back." He rubbed the back of his neck as if it'd already started to rain hell. "And something else," he said, "there are 126 City National branches in Los Angeles. We're stuck."

"Start with the main branch. Most people deposit important papers at the main branch."

"You're probably right," he said, straightening his posture. "One of these days you'll make a good detective."

Property insurance paid for all cleanup services at the *Gazette* and restored my newspaper to working order. It still smelled like smoke, but I was back in business.

I was about to write a new article on Sheriff Turnbull's investigation when he called.

"The autopsy has been approved. I thought you'd like to be here."

"When?"

"Two days. In the Greenlee morgue. Ten o'clock."

"I'll be there. And thank you."

It was gruesome. But there was nothing to learn from an X-Ray. No key in his mouth, or stomach.

She was wrong. Was she sending us on a wild goose chase?

Butch was madder than I. "Why in heaven's name did you put me through all this? What was I thinking? I don't need the key! I'm gonna find that lockbox and get a subpoena."

"Butch, I want to be there when you open it." I was serious.

He thought about my request for a second. "No."

Oneeda called a few days later, excitement in her voice. "I've got it, Martha."

"Got what?"

"The script. It took some time, but RTO sent it."

"Oh, yeah, the script from that movie. I'd forgotten about it."

With a deep tone, she let the words spill out with an eerie announcer's voice, "*The Lost Stranger*. I've read some of it. You won't believe it. I'm coming over. Let's read it together."

"Bring it," I said, hoping *The Lost Stranger* held clues to the burning of my *Gazette*.

Before we hung up, I heard a faint click. Someone had been listening in on the party line.

"Oneeda, did you hear that? The click?"

"No, I didn't hear it."

"Somebody was on our line, I'm sure of it."

"What should we do?"

"Nothing. There's nothing we can do. Come on over. Let's look at the script."

Before we sat down at the kitchen table, I asked, "How'd you get it?"

"I used some of the sheriff's stationery and wrote RTO's legal department a letter explaining how it was vital for us to get a copy of the script, as it tied in with an arson case we were investigating. I told them the clues in the movie script could be helpful. I signed it, *Deputy* Harpole."

"You did not! You're not a real—"

"I know, I know," Oneeda interrupted. "But look, it worked."

I shook my head and sat down at the kitchen table next to her.

She pulled the one-inch stack of paper from her purse. "Look who the scriptwriter was."

I took the first page from her and studied it. *The Lost Stranger. An RTO film*. "By Andy Chinn."

"There's more," she said, handing me the next page. "Look who produced it and who acted in it."

Starring Tully Ivey and Mario Mastrioni. Produced by Alston Goldsmith. Directed by Banner O'Brien. "You know what this means don't you?" Oneeda said, tapping a finger on the manuscript. "All those people working on this movie in Solo also worked on *The Lost Stranger*. Every one of them knew how to use gasoline to set fire to the *Gazette*."

"It could've been any one of them. We're back to square one."

We read the entire script, looking for clues, especially any associated with the arson scene. There were plenty of specific details about how the gasoline was used. Still, we found nothing to indicate who might have burned the *Gazette*.

16
Governor's Mansion

It couldn't have been more elegant—waiters in white jackets, weaving in and out, carrying trays of tasty meat balls, gulf shrimp, duck meat, even glasses of bubbly champagne. And the band, playing Sinatra's anthem to hell—"I Did It My Way."

Governor Bobby Barrett was a right-winged racist who hated everything black, including tuxedos. He preferred pinstriped suits.

Everybody was dressed to the hilt. Not me.

I'd taken what I could from the department's uniform closet—Khaki pants, khaki shirt, black tie, black belt. Men's stuff. But no gun. And no designer dress. I'd taken a long look at it, courtesy of Tully Ivey, and decided to wear my khakis. I wanted to look official.

I stuck like glue to Mrs. Ivey. My mission? Keep her from having a private conversation with the governor. I knew she would try to corner him, persuade him to kill the investigation. He had the power to do it.

Naturally, she was annoyed by my close presence. "Darlin', would you mind standing farther away?" she whispered into my ear. "I have fans who might not want to see me with some uniformed person shadowing my every move." She scanned me from head to toe and *tsked*. "You should have worn the designer dress I sent you."

I didn't mind her saying that. I expected it. So, I ignored it.

It wasn't long before the governor was on the microphone. His remarks about "Miss Tully Ivey" are not worth writing about. But there was one publicity coup in his closing remarks.

"Miss Ivey, as Governor of Mississippi, I want to thank you for filming your next movie in our great state."

The crowd cheered.

I wanted to blow a gasket. Partially because I knew what the movie was about. But mostly because Randy Carr was in my ear. "Deputy McRae, we would appreciate it if you would stop harassing her. She's above these things, and you know it. Let it go. Or—"

I glared at him. "Or, what?"

"You don't understand," he said. "You're from a small town. You simply haven't caught up with the ways of the new world."

"The ways of the new world?" I propped my hands on my hips. "You think just because you're from a big, sophisticated city we don't know squat down here. I'll tell you this—we know more about life than you'll ever experience. You don't know about people. You think everything's about the dollar. About making it big. Let me tell you, God didn't create us to be successful. He created us to be holy. But you wouldn't know anything about that, would you?"

"Nice speech, deputy, but I too grew up in a small California town."

Small California town was still California. Probably some surf town. No comparison.

He walked away. Immediately, I felt terrible for challenging him instead of being loving. I'd lost my temper. But it was over.

Ivey was nowhere in sight. I panicked.

I found a television reporter. "Would you like to interview Tully Ivey?"

"Yes! Of course. Is she still here?"

"Wait at the bottom of the stairs. I think I know where she is." I began searching the upstairs. Room by room. Opening a large double-door into a library, I found them, Tully Ivey and the governor, in conversation.

"Pardon me for interrupting Governor, but a television station would like her downstairs for an interview." Ivey squinted her eyes at me.

The Governor turned to her. "If you need to be somewhere else, I understand," he said. "Happens to me all the time."

"First, I'd like to know what you think about my question," she said.

"Well, Miss Ivey, I need to get back to you on that. I look forward to seeing you on TV tonight."

Tully Ivey and I left the library and began walking down the stairs. She was fuming mad at me.

"Deputy McRae, I'm going to have your job for this." When we stepped onto the mid-level landing, the TV camera lights came on. She forgot about me and descended the steps in her usual Hollywood style.

Good. Maybe I could explain The Killing to the governor before he had a chance to squash the investigation. But I'd need a plan. How could I let him know what the movie is really about? But not tonight. I needed to show him the script, which I didn't have.

The next day, Oneeda came over to brainstorm. She came up with the best idea. "We'll just send him a copy of the script. When he reads it he'll realize the harm it'll do."

"We'll need to make a copy." I rubbed my chin. "But we can't just send it. His staff will toss it."

"Either way, we gotta get the script first. It's in Chinn's room."

"And he takes it with him every time he goes out."

Getting it without Chinn knowing would be the tricky part. We sat and schemed for another hour.

We sipped a little more sherry. Then it hit me. "What about this? Let's invite Andy to a real Southern supper one night—we'll divert his attention while Mary somehow makes a copy of the script."

We agreed there was merit here. It might work.

Meantime, I needed to put another plan into action—a story in the Gazette. To write it, I needed the notes from my files. At the Gazette office, I retrieved the locked file cabinet key from my desk drawer—which got me to thinking about the missing key. Who had it? It wasn't under the window. Did it actually exist?

I quit thinking about it and concentrated on the story I was about to write—the true story of what producer Goldsmith was filming in Solo. Maybe my Gazette article would be enough to convince Governor Barrett to stop the movie.

THE GAZETTE

THE GAZETTE • TUESDAY, NOVEMBER 6, 1962

PARCHMAN MOVIE TO MAKE MISSISSIPPI LOOK BAD

"The Killing" is a new movie being filmed in the Mississippi Delta. It was supposed to be a warm-hearted movie about a beloved Solo priest, Father Adam Davidson, who was tortured and killed by an insane inmate. It seems that the producer, Mr. Alston Goldsmith, didn't "tell the whole truth and nothing but the truth" when he first arrived in Solo to explain the movie's intent to local residents. Some residents have managed to read the script and learned that the movie appears to be more about making Mississippi look like a "barbaric" state for executing death row inmate Sonny Sartain. According to those who have read the script, the movie is about the evils of capital punishment, and will make Mississippians look like bloodthirsty heathens.

That was the gist of the front-page story.

Within two days, my idea had backfired. The governor's chief of staff called. He was livid.

"How could you write such a scathing story, Mrs. McRae? Do you realize we've been after these movie companies for several years?" he shouted over the phone. "The money they bring in is significant. Just having Tully Ivey in Mississippi is good publicity. You don't seem to understand the gravity of what you've written. The governor is very disappointed."

"Mr. Rodgers, I'm investigating a murder. I'm not currently interested in the state's economic issues."

"That's too bad, because the governor is."

We hung up—with me using all the self-control I could muster not to slam the receiver in its cradle—and I thought I'd heard the end of it.

Adding insult to injury, the tabloids came out the following week, featuring Goldsmith's own version of my article.

THE HOLLYWOOD APPEAL

THE HOLLYWOOD APPEAL · THURSDAY · NOVEMBER 15, 1962

Is Mississippi Trying to Kill "The Killing?"

RTO's film, *The Killing*, staring Tully Ivey and Mario Mastrioni, is being filmed in Mississippi, for release in mid-1963. But a local deputy, who has a part in the movie, appears to be disgruntled, according to well-known producer Alston Goldsmith. Mr. Goldsmith claims the deputy also owns a local newspaper and is publishing false information about the movie.

"This deputy is using her small town newspaper to air her grievancies because she's disgruntled by a scene in which she appeared," Goldsmith claims. "She's simply not happy about the fact we cut one of her scenes. We deal with these sorts of people all the time. When the film is released, she'll be forgotten."

And the lies continued, making me look like a sour prune, a deal-killer. They hadn't even bothered to ask for my side of the story. Now I understood why Goldsmith wanted me to be an extra in that scene. He had already planned to discredit anything I published about the movie. He knew he'd run into opposition about the movie before he ever set foot in Mississippi.

Clever stinker.

That same week, I received another call from the governor's office. This time, it was the governor himself.

His voice boomed in my ear. "You've done a mighty fine job of trying to run off a new industry we've been courtin'. If these papers from Los Angeles had not of explained why you wrote that little story of yours, you just might have succeeded. But I've spoken with Mr. Hughes, the owner of RTO, about this mix up and they're going to proceed with the filming. And Mrs. McRae, I've also spoken with Sheriff Turnbull"—*uh, oh, here it comes*, I thought—"and I've instructed him to dismiss you from his department. You'll be hearing from him shortly. I just wanted you to know personally from me, as governor of this great state, how very disappointed I am in you."

He waited a few seconds for my response, but I was tongue-tied. Speechless.

"Good day, Mrs. McRae." *Click*. He was gone.

I couldn't believe my ears. I took to my bed for an entire day, ignoring all phone calls—most of them probably from Butch. I just didn't have the energy to face him.

17
The Killing

Trudging into the department the next day, I overheard Butch tell Deputy Cox, "Finally found a bank branch with deposit box number 4918. It's in Los Angeles. Here, take this to the post office. It's my request for the judge out there to issue a subpoena to that bank."

"I'm on it, sheriff," Cox said.

Butch stared out the window. "As soon as I get word on the subpoena, I'm flying out there and find out what's in that lockbox."

I approached him. "It's in the main branch, isn't it?"

"Yep, you were right."

"Butch, please, I need to be there. I'm really invested in this now. I couldn't bear not being there when it's opened. Please understand."

He studied me for a minute, pulled his broad pants up and said, "Martha, you've been a help—here and there—but I'm pulling your badge. The governor's office called and—"

"I know, I know. It's about the article I wrote."

"No joke. Why'd you do it?"

"This whole movie is about making Mississippi look bad, and the governor doesn't get it. He believes it will be good for the state."

"I have my orders. Just turn in your badge. You might as well go on home."

Taking the badge from my purse, I gently placed in on his desk. I gave him my best forlorn look, knowing I had a backup plan—Oneeda's fake badge.

Andy Chinn held up a drumstick for me to see, as if I didn't know what it was. "Mrs. McRae, this Southern dinner is *something else*. All this time I've been eating dinner with the crew, I should've been here."

"Thank you, I'm so glad you like it. We call it supper, though."

Mary and I had laid out fried chicken, mashed potatoes with gravy, fried okra, turnip greens, and a cast iron skillet of her jalapeño cornbread.

Finished with supper, Mary put her napkin aside. "Would y'all please excuse me? It's way past Michael's bedtime."

We all said goodnight to little Michael.

"Now, Andy," I said, "let's enjoy a little after-dinner sherry with Father Compañero, shall we?"

The entire caper had been pre-planned, of course.

Mary would take Michael to his room, sneak upstairs to Chinn's room, take the script over to the Gazette to mimeograph, then return the original to his room. We counted on needing an hour.

Father Paul and I left the table with all its dirty dishes and escorted Andy into the parlor for some sherry.

“Never had sherry,” he said.

“Try it. I think you’ll like it,” I said. “Not one of your new California wines, I’m sure, but, still pretty good, don’t you think?”

“Yes, I could enjoy this,” he said, taking a sip. Then added, “I’d like to thank you, Deputy McRae, for inviting me to dinner—I mean supper. This was a real Southern treat. I’ve never tasted fried okra in my life. Or turnip greens. And your cornbread—mmm—so good with that honey on it.”

“Thank you. There’s a first time for everything, right?”

“I suppose there is,” he said, sipping on more sherry.

Our job was to keep Chinn occupied until we received a phone call from Mary. All we had to do was ask about his life and let his ego take it from there.

Finally, Mary called, “It’s done,” and hung up.

I kept the phone to my ear to give Chinn the impression this was an honest-to-goodness phone call. Then I heard a second click. Someone had definitely been listening.

I returned to the parlor. “Andy, I am so sorry, I seem to be all out of sherry.”

“That’s okay, Mrs.—sorry, Deputy McRae.” He giggled like a man who couldn’t hold his wine.

We called it a night. After he trudged up the stairs, I went to Mary’s bungalow in the back of my property.

The stack of papers for *The Killing* script was more than an inch thick. I kept my tone low so no one else in the house could hear us. “There must be a hundred pages here!”

“More like a hundred and fifty.”

“Well, we best get to work. Let’s circle everything in here that proves our point to the governor.”

“You sure you’ll be able to get it to him?”

“I’ll figure something out.”

I clasped her hand before she could flip through the pages. “Mary, we have to be careful what we say on the phone. Somebody’s been listening in.”

She stared at me. “This is getting dangerous.”

“Maybe. But the sooner we get this script to him, the sooner we’ll be safe.”

We split the script into two stacks. One for each of us.

After a minute, she said, “Martha, look, here’s one of those funny c letters.”

“Let me see.” I looked at the page. “Yep, it’s all over the place. But wait. It’s not here on my pages.”

We thumbed through the entire script. Several long sections had the ç and other sections didn’t.

“What in the world is going on?” I rubbed my chin. “Several typewriters must’ve been used for the script. And we still don’t know who typed the Dawkins note.”

Early the next morning, I drove to Salem—the mimeographed

copy of *The Killing* on the seat beside me—wondering how I was going to get into the governor's office without being caught. Somehow, I'd need to bypass the hard-nosed chief-of-staff gatekeeper. If I gave it to him, he'd just toss it in the trash.

Circling the governor's residence on Capital Street in search of a parking space, I noticed tourists lined up for a tour of the mansion. Perfect.

Once inside, I slipped to the back of the line as we toured through the mansion. I could have cared less about the tour. I was only interested in the governor's library, the same one where I found him and Ivey during the party.

Ten minutes later, we gathered behind a velvet rope, looking into his personal library. The guide told some story about the library's history, and the group moved on. I hid behind a column and waited until they were out of sight, then slipped under the rope. I had to be quick, or the security guard might see me. There was only one logical place for me to deposit the script and my notes. I placed it on his leather chair, then left to catch up with the group.

As I was about to slip under the rope, a security guard appeared.

"Ma'am, the library is off limits to tourists. May I ask what you were doing?"

"Sorry, I was lost. I wandered off for a minute. Where are the restrooms in this place?"

"They're down the hall to your left. You need to go and then join up with your group."

18
Freddie

On the drive back to Solo, I wondered how I might find out when the sheriff would be flying to Los Angeles. I wanted to be there, at the bank, when he opened the lockbox.

I called Deputy Creel, the one officer I thought might help.

"Dan, I need a favor. Butch is going to be getting a letter authorizing the subpoena so the lockbox can be opened. Could you let me know when Butch is going to leave for Los Angeles?"

"You know I can't do that. Sorry, just can't."

"At least tell me if you've found out any more about Dawkins's shooting or Tully Ivey."

"No can do. Sorry, Martha. You are… how do they say it when a person has no home?"

"Persona non grata. Thanks anyway, Dan."

After hanging up, I called Deputy Washington, and asked the same questions. I received the same response. No sense calling Cox. I knew he wouldn't help.

I had nowhere to turn.

I sat at my kitchen table, praying for an answer.

One finally came. I needed to see Tully Ivey one more time. Maybe I could weasel something out of her about the key or lockbox.

When I arrived at the Grater house, Randy Carr opened the door, a grin plastered across his face. "I hear you're no longer a deputy, *Mrs.* McRae."

"You heard wrong, Mister Carr." I pulled out Oneeda's fake badge and gave him a glimpse.

"My apologies. My information must be wrong," he said. "Deputy Cox is already here, in the library with her."

"Cox is here?" I was shocked.

"Yep, she's showing him how tarot cards work. I think he's taking to it quite nicely."

I had to leave. Cox would know my real badge had been taken away.

At home, I had another idea, one that would let me know when the California judge's letter arrived in Greenlee. I called and asked my longtime friend, Freddie Carpenter, Greenlee's Assistant Postmaster, to keep an eye out for any letter addressed to the sheriff from California. I'd helped get Freddie off for murder in a mixed up fiasco three years ago when he was falsely accused of killing someone. He owed me.

One morning, two weeks later, faithful to his word, Freddie called. "Miz McRae, there's a letter here to Sheriff Butch Turnbull from a Judge Randolph Horn in California. What do you want me to do with it?"

"I need you to do what you do best. You know what I mean. Call me when you're done."

"Will do." He hung up. Before I could hang up, there was another click. Why do we have party lines? When will we have privacy here?

I waited for his call. It wouldn't take long for him to steam open the judge's letter, unless he had customers in line for stamps or something. By lunch, he still hadn't called.

Mary was home. We were eating a sandwich with Michael. I told her about the click. "Someone was listening in on my conversation with Freddie. Mary, I'm concerned about him. He hasn't called in three hours. Something could be wrong."

"It's probably nothing. People listen in all the time."

By the time I prepared supper for everyone, the phone rang. It was late afternoon. Finally, Freddie has the answer.

Instead, it was Oneeda calling. "Something terrible happened. Freddie was found near the river."

"What? Is he okay?"

"No. He's… he's gone, Martha. Gone." She was weeping.

The news knocked the air out of me, and the receiver slipped from my limp hand.

"Martha, Martha, are you there?"

I grabbed the phone from the floor and squeaked out, "What happened?"

"I only know that some kids found him on the river bank. I'm at Nelson's in Greenlee. The saleslady told me."

"I don't understand. I was just talking with Freddie this morning.

"It's terrible, I know. I'll find out what I can and get back to you. Okay?"

"Okay," I mouthed, and hung up.

I needed to get to the Greenlee post office as fast as possible. I didn't announce my departure to Mary or the rector; I just hurried to my car and took off.

A crowd had gathered around the post office, and the sheriff's cars were everywhere. I decided to walk around back and enter from the loading dock. I just needed to get into the sorting room.

Inside, Deputy Cox collected blood samples from the floor. Creel took photographs, and Butch scribbled in a notepad while holding a pair of glasses with his rubber gloves.

"Are those Freddie's glasses?"

He raised an eyebrow at me. "You're on suspension. You can't be here."

"Okay, I'll leave. Let me just grab my mail."

"Get it and go." He focused his attention back on the notepad.

I looked for the SHERIFF DEPARTMENT mail slot. There was no letter in it. I glanced around on the sly. Maybe Freddie had put it the in a drawer, or maybe it had fallen in a scuffle.

"Wait a minute." Butch frowned at me. "You don't have a mail slot in Greenlee. What are you doing? Get outta here.

Martha, I'm not gonna tell you again."

"I'm sorry, Butch. I'm just upset about Freddie. Does he have any personal effects I could see?"

"Creel, escort Miz McRae outta here. Now."

"I'm gone, I'm gone." I hustled out.

There was nothing more I could do at the post office anyway. One thing I knew for certain—whoever killed him was there to intercept the judge's order.

Poor Freddie. How could this have gone so terribly wrong?

I drove to the Yazoo River, where Freddie was found. It was roped off with yellow police tape, but no one was around. I found the shallow grave the murderer had dug for Freddie. I did a thorough search of the area. Nothing. Not even a footprint. I slipped in my car and drove home.

Oneeda came over to help with supper. Afterwards, she and I sat in the parlor and talked about Freddie and all that'd happened the last few months.

She asked, "Why would anyone want to kill Freddie?"

"I'll tell you why. Somebody didn't want the sheriff to know about the subpoena ruling."

"I'm still confused," she said. "All of this, it's so strange."

I took her back to the beginning, to Ivey's fingerprints on the note… the typewriter flaw… the lockbox subpoena … and ended with Freddie.

She seemed to understand.

"I'll call Butch tomorrow and let him know," I said. "Whoever took the letter murdered Freddie."

I changed the subject. "I'll tell you, Oneeda, I'm about worn out with everything. Between trying to figure out why Andrew was at Tully Ivey's window and now, with Freddie's murder, I don't know what to do next. But I do need to borrow that badge I made for you."

She frowned, but dug in her purse and handed it to me.

That's when the cuckoo clock struck ten. We were done for the night. On the way out, Oneeda said, "Martha, don't you remember Susie saying she'd overheard Andrew and Ivey talking about meeting at the Alamo?"

"Yes."

"Did you check the motel register?"

"Oh, no, I haven't." I felt foolish for not having thought of it myself. "Thank you for reminding me. I'll check on it tomorrow afternoon."

I already had plans for the morning.

At eight o'clock the next day, I confronted the sheriff. "Butch, I have a confession to make. May we sit in your office?"

"Oh, no. What've you done now?"

I followed him into his office. He sighed and sat behind his desk. I sat in his worn out guest chair.

"Well? Here we are. Tell me. What now?"

"I asked Freddie to intercept the judge's letter." I'd rehearsed this all the way to his office, but when the time came, all I could do was blurt it out. He dropped his jaw and gaped at me. I cringed and kept on explaining. "I wanted to know when you were going to Los Angeles. That's why I did it, Butch. I'm sorry. I'm responsible for Freddie's death. I feel awful."

He looked at me with a blank stare, not a muscle on his face moved.

Me? I peered at him with one eye open, wiping a tear from the other, hoping he'd soften up. Big men can be softies.

"I know what I did was wrong. I hope you'll forgive me. I was never going to stop the letter from getting to you. Never. I just wanted to know when you'd be going out there."

"I'm not sure whether to lock you up or let you run around with all your wild intuitions. But tell me this—how'd the killer know when the letter arrived at the post office?"

"Stupid party line. Somebody was listening in when Freddie and I talked."

"You think someone overheard you talking with Freddie and killed him? Is that what you're saying?"

"Yessir, that's what I'm saying."

"Gotta be one of the movie people," he said, shaking his head. That's a lot to cover."

I shifted in my seat, and addressed the real reason I wanted to talk to the sheriff. "I need to do one more thing before you lock me up." (Although I knew he wouldn't.) "I need to go to the Alamo and check the register. I'll bet you a steak supper that Tully Ivey spent that night with Dawkins and she's guilty of murder." I put my palm on his desk. "Let me find out if they were there. Please."

"Go. But I can't give the badge back. Governor's orders. And Martha, don't tell anybody I let you do this. Nobody. Understood?"

"Got it, sir. Thank you, Butch." I lifted up from the chair and headed toward the door, but stopped. "Oh, by the way, did you know Deputy Cox has been learning about tarot cards from Tully Ivey?"

"You're kidding me, right?"

"No sir."

I headed straight to the Alamo Motel. The same, skinny-behind, beehive bleach-blonde from three years ago was at the reception desk—Julie, according to her nametag.

"I remember you," she said, chewing some gum. "You were in here couple years ago, about that rector's murder, weren't you?"

She'd never be much help without a little push, so I pulled out Oneeda's fake badge and flashed it under her false eyelashes. "It was three years ago, not two. And now, I'm a deputy sheriff."

She glanced at it, then threw her hip out a mile and planted a hand on it. "Okay, so what'll it be this time? You want the register again?"

"Underneath the counter. Hand it to me."

Funny how rednecks never change. Still smacking on her gum, not even taking her eyes off me, she reached down and brought up the register, plopping it atop the counter. Without another word, she did a one-eighty and hightailed her proud derriere towards the back office. If only she knew how a real diva sashayed.

I opened the register and began searching through all the names from three months ago. Sliding my finger down each page, one name after another, I found only one that might be a false check-in. "A. Williamson." In the heat of the moment, Andrew Dawkins might have come up with the first name he could think of—Shirley's maiden name, Williamson. How cruel would that be?

I traced the handwriting onto a page in my pocket notebook, closed the register and said, "I'll be back."

She didn't even turn around to reply.

"Redneck," I muttered, closing the door.

I drove to Shirley's and asked to see something with Andrew's signature on it.

"Why do you need his signature?"

"I'll tell you later. Just find me something he signed. Anything. And a photo. I need a photograph of him. I'll return it, I promise."

She searched and returned a few minutes later with a bank loan document he'd signed, and a photo. I compared the signatures.

"Yes." The handwriting matched.

"What? What did you find?"

"Nothing." I couldn't tell her I'd just confirmed her husband's infidelity. "I'll talk to you tomorrow."

I thanked her and left for the Gazette, where I retrieved a file photo of Tully Ivey, then returned to the Alamo to face the beehive hairdo redneck.

"You, agin'?"

"You know, Julie, I'm willing to pay for charm school, if you're willing to go. Or do you just have a bee up there in your bonnet?"

She stepped back, halted her gum smacking, and said, "Nobody's ever talked to me like that."

"Well, somebody should have. Now, I'm going to kindly ask you to look at these photographs. That okay with you?"

She eased back up to the counter, still not sure about me.

I placed the photographs in front of her, and said in the nicest voice I could muster, "Do you recognize either of these two people?"

She started back on her chewing gum, and decided she would study the photographs.

She pointed to one. "Is this that famous actress, Tully Ivey? Yeah, that's her. I saw her sittin' in the car just outside. I thought it was her. And this man, I remember him. He's the one who checked in. What's this about? That shooting down in Solo?"

"Yes. And you just helped me. A lot. Thank you."

"Good. If you ever need a room, let me know." She twirled around and swished her hiney to the back.

Within thirty minutes, I was standing at the front door of the Grater house, rapping the knocker.

Randy Carr opened the door.

"I need to see Tully Ivey." I flashed the fake badge under his nose. "It's important."

"This has officially turned into harassment," he said. "I'm calling the sheriff and ask him why you're here, because I doubt he even knows you're here. Am I right?"

"Go ahead. Call. I'll wait."

He sighed and said, "All right. All right." Then walked away. I waited in the lobby.

Within five minutes the queen of glamour made her entrance, gracefully descending the stairs to greet me.

"Oh, dear, you again. I would have thought you'd given up on this nonsense long ago. What do you want?"

"I just need to ask one or two more questions, that's all."

She agreed to sit in the library.

Andy Chinn was in her wingback but quickly stood when he saw her. He had been using the tarot cards. She glared at him, her eyes narrowed into thin slits. He acknowledged me and left the room. Randy Carr was nowhere to be seen.

She took the wingback and gathered up the cards from the table. She flipped one over. "Ahh, the Hanged Man card."

It was colorful and full of mystical mumbo-jumbo. A man hanging upside down—only one leg holding him, the other dangling. I didn't have time to study the details, and didn't want to.

"Would you like to know it's meaning?"

"Not really." I took a seat. "I'd just like to ask you a couple of questions."

"I'll tell you anyway." She lit a cigarette and let out a steady stream of smoke. "The Hanged Man means your perspective has completely changed, and you're able to see both the mundane in this world and the spiritual."

"I have no idea what you're talking about."

"Darling, it means you've come on the right day. It means I'm open to whatever you need to know."

"Good. Here's a copy of Andrew Dawkins's signature on the register of the Alamo Motel in Greenlee. You were seen going into the motel with him three months ago. You were lovers, weren't you?"

"You say I was seen going into a motel with some man I barely knew? My dear, you must understand, everybody wants to look like me. Why, I've probably been spotted this very day in cities all over the world."

She flipped another card on the table. "Oh, my goodness, The Moon card. The querent who gets this card should be warned that they may be going through a time of emotional and mental trial, a time when they'll do things that seem to make sense to them, yet when they come out of it, they'll wonder, 'Why did I do that? It makes no sense.'"

"It makes sense to me. You shot him on purpose. I just don't understand why."

"Oh, but darling, you have no evidence. You're bluffing. The Moon card proves it."

She tamped out her cigarette and stood. "Good day, Deputy McRae. I enjoyed our little visit."

I walked out.

Well, that didn't work. Once more, I left with no answers, just the Hanged Man and Moon card on my mind—far too much for me to absorb without a glass of sherry.

I'd been to more funerals than I cared to remember. Freddie's was one of the saddest.

He was only thirty, for goodness sake.

I sat on Calvary's third row with Oneeda, Mary, Shirley, Butch, and a host of other friends. Yes, even Butch and I had a mutual understanding of our roles in Freddie's life.

I remember Father Compañero's service because I wrote a story about it in the *Gazette*.

"Only God knows our beginning and our end," he said "God is in control of everything, whether we like it or not. We need to trust the creator of the universe, or we'll end up for eternity in a place we'll regret forever. I believe Freddie was saved. But, please hear me when I say I'm not giving *advice* about Freddie's salvation—or yours—I'm giving you news. Good news. God didn't send his Son to give us advice. Advice is something we can take or leave. News is something we have to deal with." I was glad he didn't give the "He lived a good life, he's in heaven now" eulogy.

Oneeda leaned toward me. "I wish good news would visit us once in a while."

I figured the governor would soon be using his influence to persuade prosecutor Mike Wood to drop any thought of a murder charge against Tully Ivey. *Don't want to be running off the film industry, now do we?* That's how the governor would put it.

I needed to get to Wood first. The next day I called to set up an appointment.

We met in his Salem office. He was short, only five-six. He looked like an ex-Marine with a barrel chest protruding so much his tie appeared to be going over and down a waterfall to a thirty-inch waist. He had a stronger than necessary grip. No lips. And no smile.

I asked him if he had any leads on Freddie's murder. He shook his head. "No, not a single suspect. Is that why you're here?"

"No, I'm here regarding the Dawkins shooting." I pulled out my evidence and showed it all to him—the note, my written report on finding the ç on Goldsmith's now-missing typewriter, my interviews with Tully Ivey and the crew, the

Alamo manager's info about Dawkins and Ivey's relationship, the *Gazette's* burning, even my Joanna Whitfield research and kidnapping in Los Angeles. It was more than enough to convince him that Ivey should be arrested.

"I do appreciate your diligence in pursuing this matter for the state," he said with an air of military persuasion, "but you have no proof that Tully Ivey and Andrew Dawkins were having any sort of relationship. You may have what you think is his signature from the Alamo Motel, and a possible witness, but you have no solid evidence they had a relationship of any kind. And even if they did, what motive would she have to murder him? Without motive, I can't charge her with anything."

"But—"

"I will take your report under consideration and meet with my team to officially decide if we should call a grand jury proceeding. Do you have any other—"

"The governor's gotten to you, hasn't he?"

"Pardon me?" He glowered at me over his reading glasses. "Before you make an accusation like that, I think you should study the law regarding grand jury proceedings."

"I wasn't making an accusation. I was asking if the governor has spoken to you about this case. And I happen to know a great deal about grand jury proceedings."

He closed his eyes and rubbed his forehead. "Clear-cut self-defense cases rarely go to criminal trial. You should know that." He looked up at me. "I intend to telephone your sheriff and explain just how unprofessional you've been. Do you understand why?" He'd raised his voice more octaves than necessary.

"No, sir. I don't understand your logic. Not at all."

He waved me off. "That'll be all, Deputy McRae. Thank you for this report." He tossed it on his desk.

I was dismissed and dismayed, feeling like he'd disregarded every piece of evidence I had laid at his feet.

He was probably running for governor next term and wanted Barrett's endorsement.

"Lackey," I mouthed under my breath as I left his office.

19
The Meeting

I was cleaning my boarders' rooms when the phone rang. I ran down the stairs and caught it on the fourth ring. It was Harland Rodgers, the governor's chief of staff.

"The governor would like to see you as soon as possible. When can you get here?"

My adrenaline went into overdrive. "I'm not sure. I—I suppose Monday?"

"What time?"

"Hold a minute, please. I need to check my calendar." I placed the phone on the counter to gather my wits. What had Wood told the governor about my visit? Could have been anything. I'd never know unless I pursued this. I checked my calendar and picked up the phone. "I can be there at eleven Monday morning."

"He'll see you then. The guard outside will be expecting you."

"Okay."

The next day I called Butch's secretary, Cheri. She was also a friend from church. I should have thought of her before asking Creel and Washington about Butch's travel schedule.

"Cheri, it's Martha. Say, is there any news on Freddie's murder?"

"Nothing new, sweetie. Except we sure have plenty of new faces around here. The sheriff requested more deputies from Salem, what with the Dawkins' shooting, your *Gazette* fire, and now Freddie's murder. It's more than he can handle."

"I need to speak with him, but first, I need a favor."

"Anything for you, sugar."

"You may not say that when I tell you what it is."

"Try me."

"I need to know Butch's travel schedule to Los Angeles. I assume you'll be making his travel plans when the judge's letter arrives. Would you please let me know which flight he'll be on?"

I could hear her cup the speaker on the phone and whisper, "What on earth for, Martha? You're not thinking of going out there, are you?"

"Yes. On my own nickel. I'm in this up to my neck. I need to be there when that lockbox is opened. You know it wouldn't hurt for him to have a deputy with him."

She seemed reluctant, but said, "Okay, I'll see what I can do."

"Thank you. Is he there? I need to tell him something."

"Honey, he already knows. We all know. The governor wants to meet with you, right?"

"How'd you know?"

"We got word late yesterday. I'll be praying for you, Martha."

“What? Do you know something I don’t?”

“Nope. But it can’t be good if the governor calls a state employee for a private meeting.”

On Sunday, bits and pieces of Father Compañero’s sermon stuck with me. Like, “Don’t fear the one who can take your life; fear the one who can destroy both your body and your soul in hell.”

Why should I be afraid of some governor?

After church, I drove to Greenlee. Two weeks had passed since Freddie’s murder and still no suspects. I wanted to help the department. The sheriff’s office was officially in overload. With all the reinforcements, new faces, and new names, Turnbull was busy.

Seeing me, he walked over and put a hand on my shoulder. “Martha, as soon as your meeting with the governor is done, you’ll let me know what he wanted?”

“Yes, sir, I’ll call you from a pay phone. Any news from California?”

“I’ve explained everything to the judge in Los Angeles. But I’m not about to tell you when I’ll be flying out there. Besides, we don’t have the money to be sending two people across the country. We’re on a tight budget. These new hires are costing a fortune.”

“I understand.”

When he catches sight of me in Los Angeles, he’ll chew me out. Maybe take my badge.

After kitchen cleaning, I organized my notes and placed them chronologically in one of my folders. Feeling satisfied and ready for my meeting with the governor, I slipped between the sheets, tired, but unable to sleep.

I decided to have some leftover pecan pie.

Father Paul was at the kitchen table, eating what my appetite desired.

"Ahh, not able to sleep, I see," he said. "Please join me for some of your delicious pecan pie. But I must ask, you say pea-*con*, we say pea-*can*. Which is it?"

"Pea-*con*, of course." I cut a slice and sat opposite him at the table.

"Father Paul, I know you'll be honest with me. The supper I made two months ago, the Mexican dishes. Do you remember?"

"Of course I do."

"Truthfully, was it anything *at all* like what you grew up with?"

He took another bite of pie and chewed thoughtfully before answering.

"Martha," he said, gentle-like, "I love your cooking. There is nowhere I'd rather be than right here, in your home, in your kitchen, with your delicious cooking; but, I have to be honest with you. Where I come from, we had spices you don't have here in the Delta. Perhaps one day you will. Without fresh avocados, ancho chile powder, and chipotle, no one—not even the best Mexican cook—could match the exquisite taste that comes from living in that part of the world. Nevertheless, I am giving you an A for effort. It was very tasty. You simply lacked the best ingredients."

"Gee, life's like that," I said.

"Yes, it is. And may I ask, what ingredients do you have for such an important meeting tomorrow? Are you prepared?"

Father Paul was always thinking about his flock.

"Problem is, I don't know what to be prepared for." I must've looked like a lost lamb.

"Rest assured, I'll be praying for you. That's all I can do. Holy Spirit will be there with you."

"Father, you've been my favorite house guest—except for Father Davidson. You know that story, how he saved my life and all."

"Yes, I know. He was a man who comes along only once. I could never measure up to his example. I've read many of the sermons from his notebook. I wish I had his mind."

"Father Paul, you have been a true comforter to Calvary and Solo."

"And yet, Solo is still experiencing so many evil spirits," he said. "I'm concerned for my parishioners. Especially you. But I know you will do fine tomorrow." He glanced at my kitchen clock. "But for now, I must bid you good night, as I am tired and need my sleep. I hope you will forgive my lack of energy."

At five thirty, the alarm rang, same as usual. I showered, dressed, and made breakfast for everyone—a good one. Eggs over easy, crisp bacon, cheese grits, and biscuits with the always wonderful JJ's Honey. The smell of breakfast in the morning woke everybody.

Andy Chinn was my favorite breakfast eater. He never refused seconds, and always thanked me to no end.

Afterwards, Father Paul left for Calvary, Chinn for Goldsmith's Monday morning production meeting, Mary stayed to clean up, and I left for Salem, still wondering what sort of meeting I'd have with the governor.

At ten forty-five, I pulled into the governor's drive. The guard at the gate said he'd been expecting me, which did nothing to relieve my anxiety.

Chief of Staff Harland Rodgers met me at the front entrance and surprised me with a warm welcome. "Thank you for coming,"

I followed him into the main foyer, then up the circular stairway, down a hall, and through double wooden doors. The governor's high-back leather chair was vacant.

Mr. Rodgers pointed me to one of the guest chairs. "Please, have a seat. The governor will be here in a minute."

"You're staying, for the meeting?"

"Yes. I'm in most of his meetings. Would you like coffee or water?"

"Water, if you don't mind. My throat, I'm a little parched." The adrenaline had left my mouth feeling like cotton.

He walked to the wet bar ten feet away, poured water from a lead-crystal carafe, and brought me a full glass. The governor entered from a side door—a tall man with broad shoulders, a large face, and jowls that bobbed up and down. He was hunched over a bit, maybe from the civil rights riots, the likely burden on his shoulders.

"Mrs. McRae, good to finally meet you," he said with enthusiasm. "May I offer you some—oh, good, I see Harland has gotten you a glass."

He approached, I stood, and he engulfed my hand in his own. "Good of you to come, good of you to come."

He took a seat. Leaning over his desk towards me, hands clasped together, he looked me in the eye and said, "Mrs. McRae, do you know why I've asked to meet with you today?"

"No, sir, I don't."

"Let's just say I'm a believer now. I'm guessing—correctly, I hope—that it was you who left this movie script in my library." He held it up in the air for me to see. "How you were able to sneak into my library is not why I invited you here. That's a concern I'm taking up with my security detail. But… but, I did read it. Along with your notes. Most intriguing, I must say. It was you who left this, wasn't it?"

"Yes, sir. I—I didn't know how else to—"

He held up a large right palm to stop me. "Say no more. I

understand why you went to great lengths to get this in my hands." Tightening his sagging jowls, he looked over at his chief of staff. "Mr. Rodgers here evidently blocked your earlier efforts to bring this to my attention, and he's paying the price for his ineptness, I assure you."

Rodgers hadn't budged an inch. He looked bankrupt, devoid of expression.

Turning his attention to me, the governor said, "Now, let's get down to business. As we speak, our great state is going through hell and back right now, what with all this Meredith business at Ole Miss. Hell, Bobby Kennedy is all over my—excuse me—my rear end. Our great state doesn't need any more of this ugly publicity. And a movie like this,"—he held up the script again—"I won't stand for any more of this negative national news. We don't need any more manure written about our state. I commend you for bringing it to my attention."

I managed to hold off a big grin.

"Now, Mrs. McRae, I realize I made a little mistake when I had that sheriff of yours rescind your badge, and I offer my sincerest apologizes for that. But right now, I want you to get back up there. Find out what's going on with this movie business. Here's my personal phone number in case you need to call." I accepted his card with a smile. "Oh, and I encouraged the state's DA to proceed with a case against Mrs. Ivey. Lord knows, I don't want to cause her any harm, but we must stop this movie from going any farther. You do understand?"

I didn't have a chance to respond to the governor before the double doors opened. I turned to look.

"Come on in, Mike." The governor waved my attention to the stern military man strutting through the door. "I want you to meet Mike Wood, one of our great state's District Attorneys."

I stood to shake his hand. "Mr. Wood and I've already met."

"That's right, Governor. On another matter," Wood said.

He was lying through his teeth. I'd met with him for the sole purpose of turning all my evidence over to him on this very case. *Political ambition* was the phrase that came to mind.

"Good," Governor Barrett said. "I expect you to work with him in any and all requests he may have. I want a trial and I want you to help Mr. Wood shut this movie production down. Do I make myself clear to both of you?"

I glanced at Wood to see what he would say. He gave a stiff, military nod.

I faced the governor. "Yes, sir. But, may I ask a question?"

"Of course."

"Your lockbox at City National bank. It's number 4918. You have the same deposit box number that was mentioned in Andrew Dawkins's note to Tully Ivey."

None of us were certain that the Los Angeles lockbox number 4918 contained the note. It could still be in Salem—in the governor's box.

"I have no idea what you're talking about." He stared at me without a wince.

I stood there, wracking my brain—should I ask him if I could look inside 4918?

"What's your point?" Wood barked at me.

"Oh, nothing. Probably just a coincidence." Though I didn't believe in them.

After the meeting, I called the sheriff from a pay phone to give him the good news. I told him how the governor had given me his personal phone number, "in case I need to call him." I felt like a real deputy again. Turnbull's "humph" indicated he didn't share my joy.

Back home, after supper, Father Compañero and I sat in the parlor.

"Father Paul, I've told you everything I know about the missing key, the lockbox, Tully Ivey, Freddie Carpenter… all of it. What advice can you give me? I'm at a loss for what to do next."

He sighed. "Martha, Martha, you worry too much. Trust in the Lord. Trust he'll lead you in the right direction. Personally, I have no idea what you should do."

That night, I was on my knees, praying, talking with God, searching for answers.

20
Guilty

Why did I wake with such guilt? I thought he was going to answer my prayers, give me direction, tell me what to do. No, I woke from a terrible dream about Freddie's murder and my part in it. If only I hadn't asked him to steam open that judge's letter he might still be alive.

I needed to confide in someone.

After breakfast, I told Father Paul how guilty I felt.

"Satan *wants* you to feel guilty," he said. "Satan is the ultimate accuser. He cherishes our guilt. Do you know why? Because our guilt leads us away from realizing God's sovereignty. Guilt is like telling God you don't trust his promises. Guilt makes us believe we're in control, not God."

"But still, if I hadn't involved Freddie, he'd still be alive."

"God wanted him to come home. It was time."

"But you didn't know him. How do you know he went to heaven?"

"Good question. I don't. And you're right, I didn't know Freddie that well. But Martha, here is a difficult, yet truthful understanding we should all know about our creator. There are people destined for destruction, so that those who are chosen for eternal life will have gratitude, knowing what God has done for *them.* If everybody went to heaven, what gratitude could anyone possibly have for the very God who saved them? Read Romans chapter nine. It's all there. My namesake, the Apostle Paul, explains it very clearly."

"Wait, you're talking about something way over my head. I was talking about feeling guilty."

"Unless you realize God's unconditional love for us, even the sacrifice of his own son, you'll never understand why he doesn't want his children to carry guilt around forever."

As he stood to retrieve his coat, I said, "I'd like to know more about God's sovereignty. I have a difficult time believing we're puppets, without free will to choose for ourselves."

"Oh, we have free will, Martha. Just like God gave Adam and Eve free will," he said, reaching for his coat. "We're free to do whatever we want. And we're free to accept his salvation, or we can dismiss it. Here's what we must realize. God is not part of our story. We're part of his."

He slid his arms into his coat and looked at his watch. "I'm sorry, but I need to run. I have a meeting in five minutes at the church. Can we talk later?"

"Of course," I said. "I don't suppose you'd tell me if you're meeting with Tully Ivey, would you?"

"I can't say. I'm sure you understand."

Butch phoned the next day. "Martha, the governor called and wants you reinstated as deputy. Come in today."

After I got my badge back, I asked Butch if there were any new leads in Freddie's murder.

"All we know is that he was struck over the head with a blunt instrument. His skull was cracked." I winced at his graphic description. Butch was not one to hold back his raw thoughts. He was all Marine.

"We haven't found the murder weapon. And we haven't found a suspect," he said.

"Nothing from the movie crew?"

"They all have alibis."

"I have an idea, if you'd allow me."

"I'll listen. We got nothin' else to go on."

"If it was someone from the crew, they would've overheard my conversation with Freddie when I asked him to steam open the letter. Have you checked with the switchboard operators? Maybe they know who was on the party line at that time."

"Good thought, but there's no way they can keep up with the switches. Too much phone traffic."

"What about vehicles? All the crew people have rentals. Any witnesses see their cars at the post office?"

"I swear, one day you might make a good detective; but, that's a waste of time. Nobody would remember all the cars."

"Why don't you let me check on it?" I said. "Remember, I

arrived at the post office shortly after it happened. Maybe if I look at your photos I can recognize some of the folks who were there. Maybe somebody saw one of their cars."

"You go right ahead. I'm at a loss. Have at it."

I was pleased to see Butch coming around to my way of thinking.

First I needed to identify all of the crew's vehicles. There were only two rental places in Greenlee. I guessed that all of the crew probably had rented from the same company. I struck pay dirt with my first call. Three cars had been rented from Avis. But they were all registered in the name of Alston Goldsmith. It would be hard to pin Freddie's murder on any of them.

After getting the description of each vehicle, I sat at my police desk and poured over photos taken at the post office by the deputies. I recognized a few faces in the crowd and called them. "Do you remember any of the following vehicles being parked out front of the post office that day?" I rattled off a description of the three rental cars.

Nobody knew anything. I wasn't surprised.

What if the murderer had parked in the rear of the post office, near the loading dock? Problem was, nobody would have been back there to see any car.

With my mind so full of conundrums and contradictions, I felt like flailing away on a county fair whack-a-mole contraption.

Instead, I decided to sit alone in my parlor and wait for my cuckoo clock to strike five so I could calm my nerves with a glass of sherry. When the bird popped out and "cuckooed" five times, I not only poured myself a glass, I also realized why they're called cuckoo clocks. They drive you crazy.

I wondered if Mary was still at the church. I called.

She answered, "Calvary Episcopal Church. May I help you?"

"Mary, it's me. And yes, you can help me. I hope. But you'll have to do something that may require forgiveness on your part."

"Oh, I like the sound of this already," she whispered. "What is it?"

"I need to sort of accidentally bump into Tully Ivey after she comes out of her next meeting with Father Paul."

"What if she doesn't come back?"

"She'll be back, I'm sure of it."

21
Motive

One week later, Mary called from Calvary.

"She's here now," she whispered, then hung up.

I walked over to the church and sat on a bench next to the only car in the lot with a rental sticker. I imagined Tully Ivey in Father Paul's office, just the two of them.

Thirty minutes later, she walked out of the church's side door. I stood and pretended to be walking in to see the rector.

"What a coincidence, ma'am. I was just going in to see Father Paul, too," I said.

"What makes you think I was here to see him, darling?"

"I'm sorry, I just assumed—"

"I like to visit churches when I'm on location. It helps me get a better feel for the script."

"Well, you picked a good church to explore." I tilted my head to the side, trying to look innocent. "Ma'am, would you mind if I asked a personal question?"

Tully Ivey reached for the door handle of her car. I moved closer and placed my hand over hers. I smiled. "It'll only take a minute. Maybe we could both just sit in the car and talk. Would you do that with me?"

"Is this official business?"

"No, actually not."

"Get in," she said.

I walked around to the passenger door, wondering if she would try to twist my mind into something I'd regret, like Father Paul had said. My senses went on high alert. By the time I slid into the car, she was already puffing on a freshly lit cigarette.

"So what is your question, deputy?"

"Like I said, I just want to get to know you better."

"Know me better? Like what?"

"Start with your childhood."

She took a long drag from her cigarette and blew out the smoke. "Okay, I don't mind telling you." She placed both hands on the steering wheel, the cigarette holder nestled between her fingers. "For one, I never knew my parents. They gave me up to a Catholic orphanage. But I'm sure you already know that," she said, turning to face me. "I did meet with Father Compañero, and I'm going to assume he told you everything about me."

"No-no, that's not true," I said. "He only told me a little bit."

"You're lying, dear. But if you want to know about me, I'll tell you. I was a screwed up teenager living under the tyranny of strict nuns and a perverted priest. I ran away at age sixteen, headed for Hollywood. I wanted nothing more than to be famous. To be rich. To be free to do whatever I wanted. And I did. Now here I am, rich and famous."

"To me, that's sort of sad."

"Sad? Look at you. Look at me. I made it. I'm happier than ever. You're just a—no, I won't say that. You're probably happy doing what you do. But part of you wishes you were me. Don't you?"

"Truthfully, part of me does, yes. I have to admit. Being catered to. Having everybody swoon over you. It has to be an exciting life."

"What are you after, deputy? What's really on your mind?"

"I just wanted to get past the veneer, and find out who you really are."

She raised her hands above the wheel. "I'm me. Right here, flesh and blood. I'm Tully Ivey."

"Something tells me—call it instinct—there's a part of you that misses not having a normal childhood. Tell me I'm wrong."

She took long puff and blew it out the window. She'd lost that confident, glorious smile. "I see Father Compañero told you more than you're letting on. But never mind. It's true. I didn't have a pleasant life when I was younger. I was paraded around in little girl beauty contests. When I turned fourteen men just wanted a piece of me. My priest even raped me. What would you do? Would you want men to own you, or would you rather own them?"

"Neither," I answered. "I was married for twenty-one years. It was a marriage of mutual respect. I wouldn't trade that for anything." I misted over just a tad, hoping, wanting her to like me, trust me. Besides, like my father always said, when a soldier gave false information to the enemy, it wasn't lying, it was acting. I was acting.

She sighed. "I'm sorry. I'll bet you never married again, did you?" She seemed sincere.

"Nope. There's never been a man who could measure up to Shorty." I looked out the window, spending a moment reminiscing, then turned to face her. "Besides, I was never asked."

Her tone changed. "Keep it that way. You're better off not being tied down. Take my word for it. Men only want one thing, and it's not love. They'll use you and toss you like trash."

I felt sorry for her, but really wanted her to trust me. "You know, it just dawned on me … you probably didn't shoot Andrew Dawkins on purpose. You didn't have a good enough reason to shoot him, did you?"

"Darling, that's what I've been saying all along. Yes, I knew him. Problem was, he started to remind me of my priest. The one who raped me. I'm sure Father Paul told you about it." Her gaze met mine and she waited for a response.

Instead, I stayed with her confession so I could learn more. "Why did Andrew remind you of your priest?"

"Like I said, he raped me. He thought I was his property. He thought he owned me."

Tully Ivey must've realized she divulged too much. She tried to cover it—"What I meant to say is that Andrew became like all the men in my life."

"What I don't understand is why he had that note in his hand. It doesn't make sense."

"No it doesn't," she said. "And your job is to get inside that lockbox and find out what it's all about. It seems to me whatever's in there could clear up this mess about Rod Russell. I can't believe the sheriff hasn't done it yet."

I didn't tell her the Sheriff had likely located the deposit box in Los Angeles. "We're working on it. It's not easy without the key."

"Well, keep looking." She inserted the car key into the ignition. "Unless there's something else you need to ask me?"

"No, that's all. Thank you for talking with me. I appreciate getting to know you a little better."

"Au revoir," she said in excellent French, cranking the engine.

"I remember the movie where you said that! You played a French woman who'd been jilted by her lover."

"That's right. *French Nights*, 1947." She winced. "Not my best performance."

"Then, in the end, you shot and killed the leading man, and used that same French phrase as you stood over his body."

"That's right. 'Au revoir.' I actually made the director change the ending. I couldn't let the man who used me get away with that, could I?"

"I guess not."

I opened the door and slid out. Closing it, I looked back in through the window to thank her, but she was already pushing the gas petal.

I didn't sense that any part of my mind had been twisted. Not at all.

Out of the blue, it hit me. That was the second time she referred to the note in Dawkins's hand, and not once had she said anything about Andrew loving her. She'd only been interested in the lockbox. Hmmm.

Butch should know right away what Tully Ivey told me.

"Orv-wär? What's that mean?"

"It means goodbye, farewell," I said.

"So, you think she's capable of shooting Dawkins in cold blood and simply saying goodbye?"

"Yes. Like I told you, she claimed Andrew reminded her of the priest who raped her. I really do think Andrew raped her. I hate to say it. Fact is, she hates men. You can tell by the way she talks about them. Yet, she needs to control them. She has a real aversion to men who get too close."

"Too close?"

"You wouldn't understand. Let me give you an example. Twice now, I've heard her reference the note in Andrew's hand, and not *once* has she mentioned the part where he says he loves her."

"I don't believe it. You've just laid out a decent profile of this woman; and you may have uncovered a motive."

"Butch, it's all just a theory."

"But a pretty good one." He turned toward his assistant and yelled, "Cheri, Get Mike Wood on the phone."

Butch and Wood talked for a few minutes, then Butch hung up.

"What'd he say?"

"He said we have a motive. He thinks she can be charged with murder. He's going to confer with the governor first."

"I'm not surprised about that."

22
Tully Ivey's Arrest

Three days later, Butch had the arrest warrant tucked beside him on the seat of his patrol car. Three deputy cars followed us to the Grater house.

The sheriff knocked and Andy Chinn opened the door.

Butch wasted no time. "Where is she?"

"She's in the library, but it's not a good time to disturb her."

Butch didn't even acknowledge him; he shouldered him aside and walked into the foyer. We followed to the library. She was studying tarot cards as we walked in.

"Well, Sheriff Turnbull… and Deputy McRae… and, oh my, all of you! What's the occasion?"

"Tallulah Ivey, you're under arrest for the murder of Andrew Dawkins. Here's the arrest warrant. You need to come with us."

Once a queen, always a queen. She stood and twirled around, ever so slowly, like Frances Farmer in *Come And Get It*. She gathered her hands behind her back, twisted her head over her shoulder, and said,"Sheriff, I can't tell you how embarrassing this is going to be for Mississippi."

"Put your hands away. I'm not handcuffing you. You're just going to come along with us."

She turned to face the sheriff. "What? No handcuffs?"

He snatched a pair of cuffs from his belt, and rattled them. "I don't think you'd look too good in a photograph with these on." He shoved the handcuffs back in its pouch.

Butch and I drove her to the Greenlee jail. She was out on bond before the sun sank.

I'd been expecting Mike Wood's call since Tully Ivey's arrest.

"Mrs. McRae, this is Mike Wood. I realize that I dismissed your report when we met, but I'm not going to apologize (*No surprise there*), because, frankly, I'm not one-hundred percent certain she's guilty."

I quickly replied, "If you're not convinced, then why'd you bring charges?"

"I'd rather not go into that just now. Nevertheless, I am preparing for Tully Ivey's grand jury proceeding. I need to collect some information from you. Could you meet me in my Salem office, say, day after—"

"I apologize for interrupting, but would you mind meeting me here in Solo? I have a great deal on my plate, and well, I'd like to show you Solo. It could help in your proceedings."

I admit, I wanted to meet Wood on *my* turf this time, something my sweet Shorty taught me long ago. 'A bull-headed person will always have more bull if he's in his own pasture'.

“I’m afraid that’s not possible. My schedule is tight. I’ve already completed most of my discovery. At this point, I just need to interview you and a few others.”

He was mighty headstrong. But so was I. “I’ll bet you didn’t visit Calvary Church and meet our rector, Paul Compañero, did you?”

“Why should I? Does he have something to offer in this case?”

“Maybe. There’s a lot you could learn from him.” I was thinking of Father Paul’s knowledge of her.

There was an eternity of silence between us. “Okay, Mrs. McRae. I’ll come to you. When?”

“Tomorrow afternoon around two would work for me. Is that okay with—”

“I’ll see you then.” *Click.*

I didn’t think Mr. Wood cared much for me. And I wasn’ sure he’d picked up on my subtle hint that Father Paul might have some important information to share about Ivey.

I called Father Paul at the church office. “I hope you’ll forgive me. I’ve sort of obligated you to something.”

“Oh, what’s that?”

“To meet the prosecutor handling the Ivey case. He’ll be here tomorrow afternoon.”

“Martha, Martha, what have you gotten me into? What could he and I possibly talk about?”

“You might tell him some things about Tully Ivey.”

"There's nothing else to tell."

"You could witness to him. I don't think he's seen the light."

"That sounds like something Oneeda would say."

"You're right. It does. Okay, when he gets here, I'll just tell him you're out of town."

"No, no, don't lie. I'll be here tomorrow. Just send him over." The resignation in his voice was unmistakable. Suddenly, I felt terrible for putting him in such an awkward situation.

"I am so sorry. I realize I shouldn't have asked you. I don't know what I was—"

"It's okay. If it helps you, I'll do it. Just please call before he comes."

"I will. I apologize about this."

"It's okay, Martha. You can make up for it with some fried chicken and cornbread."

The following afternoon, I was frying chicken parts and making jalapeño cornbread, when the doorbell rang.

I opened the door to a sour Mike Wood.

Scanning my apron, he asked, "Is this what you call busy?"

Patience, Martha, I reminded myself.

"Oh, this is just one of many things I do." I removed my apron and led him toward the parlor, talking along the way. "Besides having the newspaper to write and print, I run a boarding house, and I cook two meals a day for my renters. But I'm sure your calendar is as full as mine, so I really do appreciate your traveling here to meet." And I meant it—I wanted him in my pasture.

He slipped out of his overcoat and draped it over a chair.

"Would you like something to drink? Tea? Coffee?"

"Coffee. I don't have much time, so if it's not already made, please don't bother."

"Oh, I always have coffee on. I'll be right back. You take sugar or cream?"

"Black."

In the kitchen, I filled two cups—one for him, one for me—then hurried back. He gave it a tentative sip, then nodded his approval, and we sat.

He leaned forward, cradling the porcelain saucer in his hands. "Mrs. McRae, I'd like to get right down to business." He placed the saucer and cup on the table and retrieved an object from his briefcase. "This is a recording device. Do you object to being recorded?"

"No, not at all, Mr. Wood."

I thought he'd ask me to call him Mike, but he didn't.

He spoke clearly and distinctly into the device. "This is Mike Wood, District Attorney for the state of Mississippi. Today is Tuesday, January 8, 1963, the time is fifteen hundred hours. I'm in the home of Deputy Martha McRae, a potential witness in the grand jury proceeding regarding Mrs. Tallulah Ivey." Pausing for a second, he said, "Mrs. McRae, I'd like to begin by asking you to explain your involvement in the Andrew Dawkins shooting." He set the recorder on the table. "Just speak normally. The recorder can hear you."

"Let's see, where to begin? Of course, you know I already told you most of this in your office. And you have my report."

"You did. But I prefer to work my cases from recordings."

"Well, in that case…" I stretched forward towards the recorder, not believing it could pick up my voice, "I guess I should start with Shirley Dawkins's call that night. She asked if I'd go to the sheriff's department and find out what happened to Andrew."

I continued with the entire story—everything from the tape on the note, Ivey's fingerprints on it, the missing key, the letter ç, Goldsmith's typewriter, my near-death experience in Los Angeles, and the Rod Russell witness—Joanna Whitfield.

"So, do you have any idea where the key is?"

"I have no idea."

"Now, go back to your meeting with Mrs. Ivey when the two of you were in her car, talking. What did she say about Andrew Dawkins?"

I told him everything.

Finished, I picked up my cup and took a sip." I'm going to give you a heads up, Mr. Wood. If she ever goes to criminal trial, you'll have a difficult time trying to keep her from wrapping the jury around her little finger. She's a professional charmer."

"Thank you for the warning, but I've been doing this for five years. Besides, I've already spent plenty of time with her."

"Oh, really? Do you think she's guilty?"

"It's not for me to decide. It'll be up to the grand jury. And then a criminal jury if there's a trial."

"I understand. But do you believe she's guilty?"

"My job is to discover the evidence to its fullest extent, present it properly, and let the jury decide." He checked his watch, stood, and said, "Thank you for your time and for the coffee."

"Oh, I thought you might want to meet our rector, Paul Compañero, at Calvary."

"Why should I meet with him?" He reached for his overcoat.

"He might give you some insight into her. Into Tully Ivey."

"Like I said, I've already met with her. I know enough. Good day, ma'am."

"Will you be calling me as a witness?"

"You can count on it, Deputy McRae."

As he walked to his car, briefcase in hand, I yelled, "Mr. Wood, will you ever run for governor?"

He twirled around, stared at me for a second, and said, "Maybe." He slid in his car seat and drove away.

I hope not.

I called Father Paul at the church.

"You're off the hook. The DA left. Went back to Salem. Said he'd call if he needed you for the grand jury proceedings."

"Good. By the way, I won't be at supper. I'm preaching tonight in Summerville."

One thing about Father Compañero, he wasted no time in spreading the Word over the Delta—little towns, little churches, all without a full-time minister. Denominations didn't matter to him. He was constantly preaching somewhere on Sunday nights.

One week later, I received a certified letter requesting me to testify in Greenlee for a grand jury proceeding. The State of Mississippi versus Tallulah Ivey. Murder in the first degree.

I had six weeks to think about this.

23
The Grand Jury

Sheriff Butch Turnbull, the medical examiner, and I were the only witnesses, and for good reason. In grand jury proceedings, the prosecution never wants to divulge more of their case than necessary. They don't want the defense knowing everything about their strategy should the defendant go to criminal trial. But still, enough evidence was needed to persuade the grand jury to vote for a criminal trial. Otherwise, the accused goes free.

The only people allowed in these proceedings are the prosecutor, the jury, the court reporter, and the witnesses. The defendant can't attend. Not even a judge.

Mike Wood approached the jurors, introduced himself, and gave instructions. "Ladies and gentlemen, I want to stress that grand juries are impaneled for the sole purpose of deciding if there is *probable cause* to believe a person committed a crime. The defendant, Tallulah Ivey, has been charged with first-degree murder, which means you will decide—not her guilt or innocence—but whether she should be tried in criminal court. Today, you'll hear evidence presented only by me, the prosecutor. Raise your hand if you have any questions regarding your duty."

Nobody raised a hand.

Wood asked the medical examiner and me to step out into the hallway as he called Sheriff Turnbull to the witness stand. The new rules in grand jury proceedings stated that no witness could be in the courtroom when another witness gave testimony.

I sat on a hallway bench with the medical examiner and imagined Butch answering Wood's questions, likely telling him about the shooting and Ivey's fingerprints on the note found in Dawkins's hand.

Forty-five minutes later, Butch stepped out and sat next to me. When the medical examiner was called, I turned to Butch. "What questions did he—"

"Stop right there," Butch said. "We're not allowed to discuss our testimony with anybody."

A few minutes passed and I said, "Well, tell me this. Did you find out what Cox was doing at the Grater house, playing with those tarot cards?"

"I told him he was never to go there again without my permission."

"How'd he take it?"

"Like a man. Which is more than I can say for you." He grinned. Butch had a funny way of expressing himself.

Thirty minutes passed and the medical examiner came out. It was my turn.

The prosecutor told me to raise my right hand and place my left on a Bible. Then he rattled off the oath question.

"Do-you-swear-to-tell-the-truth-the-whole-truth-and-nothing-but-the-truth-so-help-you-God?"

"I do."

"Please state your name."

"Deputy Martha McRae.

"You may be seated."

Prosecutor Wood stepped to the witness box. "Deputy McRae, exactly what did the defendant tell you that caused you to believe she was guilty of murder?"

"She told me that Andrew Dawkins had raped her."

"What else did she tell you?"

"She said Andrew Dawkins reminded her of the priest who had raped her when she was in the orphanage. She said, 'He's like all the other men who think I'm their property.'"

Wood asked about my other meetings with Ivey. I told him everything, reading from the notes I'd taken after each encounter. And I told him about the tarot cards.

"It's all hogwash," I said.

"What's hogwash?"

"The tarot cards. They're evil. It's witchcraft."

Wood smiled towards the jury, then faced me again. "Do you know what RTO Studios and Tully Ivey have been doing in Mississippi?"

"Of course I do. They've been filming a movie. *The Killing*."

"Oh, right, the true story of Sonny Sartain's execution."

"True my foot. There's nothing true about it."

"Why do you say that?"

"I read the script. It makes Mississippians look like uneducated ignorants for executing the most evil man I'd ever met."

Wood spun towards the jury, nodding in agreement with my assessment.

I took a breath and glanced at the jurors. Most Mississippians don't take lightly to being dismissed as uncivilized. I happen to know families who proudly display needlepointed pillows inscribed with the words, *It's hard to be humble when you're from Mississippi.*

"Deputy McRae, were you paid to be an extra in the movie?"

"I was, but I refused payment."

"And what did you learn from your experience as an extra?"

I told Wood everything I'd found wrong about their execution scene.

The proceedings lasted only two hours. Wood stepped out into the hallway and told us he was confident the jury would vote for a true bill—the official declaration of probable cause.

Butch and I headed to Charlie's place for some barbeque to wait on the jury's verdict.

At two o'clock, the call came.

Butch took the call, then strutted back to our booth, smiling with the news. "She's going to criminal court."

"And the date for the trial? Did they give a date?"

"Nope. It'll be months before any trial. Meanwhile, we need the judge in Los Angeles to issue the bank subpoena so we can get in that lockbox."

"What's taking so long?"

"They're having trouble issuing a second subpoena. Evidently, it's a new judge. He's never issued the same one twice. Says it's our problem."

"Our problem? That's ludicrous. How could it be our problem?"

"I know. I'm working on it."

"And Freddie? Still no leads?"

"Nothing. Not even a murder weapon."

The next week we received word on the trial date: July eighth, four months away. All the movie worker-bees left for Los Angeles. Only the bigwigs and Andy Chinn stayed.

Oneeda told me Ivey's attorney had visited the Grater house on several occasions.

"Probably prepping his witnesses for the trial," I said.

24
The Trial

Finally, July seven appeared on my kitchen calendar. Mary made supper that night. I was too preoccupied with the day ahead, concerned the jury wouldn't believe my story.

RTO had dispatched their California lawyers to Greenlee and hired the highest paid trial lawyer in Mississippi, the one who would ultimately defend Tully Ivey—Frank Acuff, former prosecutor for the state. Acuff was now in private practice, making a killing defending wealthy clients. Tall, lanky, in his late thirties, he had the look of an FBI man in black suit, white shirt, and thin black tie.

To say the courthouse was a circus wouldn't do justice to the chaos. There were a dozen reporters in fedoras snapping photographs of everybody entering the building.

Bethel County farmers—friends of Andrew, I assumed—carried signs and shouted, "No More Hollywood" and "Justice for Dawkins!" We were officially in the national news.

Inside the dark, wood-paneled courtroom, lazy ceiling fans tried their best to circulate the hundred degree July air. A Mississippi and an American flag flanked the judge's empty chair.

There was so much hubbub that Oneeda, Mary, and I could barely hear each other. It took ten minutes for everyone to settle.

We sat near the aisle, fourth row, behind the prosecution's table. Shirley sat in front of us, directly behind the prosecutor. She was dressed in all black.

The diva of drama made her appearance from a side door. She looked as feminine as ever, with her perfectly contoured face and red hair up in a simple bun. Her ensemble was the most striking I'd ever seen in any magazine. Not sophisticated, just elegant, yet understated. She walked erect, her head held high, with no expression. She couldn't have looked more innocent. She had perfected that look in a Hitchcock movie. I couldn't remember which one. Neither could Oneeda.

Ivey sat at the defendant's table, surrounded by her California lawyers and Frank Acuff. Randy Carr was two rows behind them. The RTO executives were spread out, not sitting together.

The bailiff entered and shouted, "All rise!"

Judge Clarence Chapman and his long black robe entered from a side chamber. After he sat, the bailiff resumed. "Hear ye, hear ye, the Circuit Court of Bethel County is now in session, the Honorable Clarence Chapman, Circuit Judge presiding. All persons having business before this court come forward and you shall be heard. No hats in the courtroom. God save the great State of Mississippi and this honorable court. Be seated."

The court clerk stood and read: "The State of Mississippi versus Tallulah Ivey, on the charge of first-degree murder."

Judge Chapman addressed Acuff. "How does the defendant plead?"

"Not guilty, Your Honor."

"Is the prosecution ready to proceed?" Chapman asked Mike Wood.

"We are, Your Honor."

"And the defense?"

Acuff answered, "We are, Your Honor."

Opening a notebook, the judge addressed Wood. "The prosecution may begin with an opening statement followed by the defense."

Prosecutor Wood stood and walked toward the jury. "Ladies and gentlemen, Mississippi law requires that first-degree murders include three basic elements—willfulness, deliberation, and premeditation. Over the course of this trial, the State of Mississippi intends to prove that Tallulah Ivey willingly and deliberately shot and killed Andrew Dawkins with premeditation. We will prove to you that she was lying in wait for Mr. Dawkins on that dreadful night of August tenth, 1962.

"Most importantly, I will present the defendant's motive. To put it bluntly, ladies and gentlemen, Mrs. Ivey had a hatred for men who had taken advantage of her. She told a law enforcement officer that Andrew Dawkins had raped her, and she wanted revenge. She invited him to her bedroom window that night. She shot and killed him in cold blood."

Wood paced in front of the jury, regarding each of them individually. "Now I want you to keep in mind that if she truly thought someone was at her window to do harm to her, she could easily have run and received help from the four men sleeping upstairs. I believe that's what each of you would have done. But she didn't. Why? Because she *planned* to kill him."

Mike Wood kept pouring it on for another ten minutes, then returned to his desk.

It was Frank Acuff's turn to address the jury.

"Ladies and gentlemen, by August 10, 1962, Tallulah Ivey had already been traumatized. She'd been accosted and beaten by a man in Los Angeles. She was a woman who now feared for her life."

He continued. "I hope you'll keep her frame of mind forefront in your thoughts as I now take you back to the very night of August tenth, one year ago. The defendant is in her bedroom, reading the movie script, memorizing her lines, when she hears something outside. Scared out of her mind, she takes her legally-owned pistol from the bedside drawer, and walks toward the window. A stranger was trying to break in.

"My client, Tallulah Ivey, was merely protecting her own life. She did what any woman would do. She fired the pistol.

"Ladies and gentlemen, I'm a Mississippian. I own a pistol. And you have many friends who do. Don't you think your friends would have done the same to protect *their* lives? Wouldn't you? Would you let someone break into your bedroom and wrestle that weapon away from you? He might kill you!

"Tallulah Ivey was simply protecting her life. She shot a man trying to enter her bedroom," he said. "I even intend to prove Andrew Dawkins was *stalking* her. He had no business being at her bedroom window at midnight on August tenth."

I peeked at Shirley. She had dropped her head in her hands, sobbing.

Acuff continued. "And you—a jury of eight men and four women—have the burden of deciding if she is guilty. That means you must believe, *beyond a reasonable doubt*, that she shot and killed Andrew Dawkins deliberately and willfully with premeditation. Yet, you will hear no eyewitness testimonies today. This case should never have been brought to trial.

"You alone have the burden of deciding whether the state of Mississippi should send her to the execution chamber, or if she can go back to making movies."

He was done.

At eleven o'clock, Judge Chapman told Wood to call his first witness. He called Sheriff Butch Turnbull.

"Sheriff Turnbull, how long have you been the sheriff of Bethel County?"

"Nine years this May."

"And before that, what did you do?"

"I was a Marine MP, stationed in Korea."

"And what does MP stand for?"

"Military Police."

"Now, I'd like to ask you some questions about that night, the night of August tenth, last year."

Wood inquired about the pistol, the wound Dawkins had received, the RTO men at the scene, and finally about the note found in Dawkins's hand.

Turnbull answered all the questions.

Then Wood handed him the note. "Can you identify what this is?"

"Yes, this is the note I found in Mr. Dawkins's hand."

Wood approached the bench and handed it to Judge Chapman. "Your Honor, I move to introduce this as Exhibit A."

Acuff approached. The judge and Acuff agreed to allow it.

Wood took the note back to Turnbull. "Sheriff, would you read it so the jury can hear what it says?"

Butch cleared his throat and read from the note. "'Tully, I don't deserve you. The short time we had together will always be with me. I will always love you. I just want you to know the proof of your innoçençe in the Rod Russell shooting is in lockbox 4918 at City National Bank. One day I will explain why I didn't tell you earlier. The key is on the ledge. Andrew.'"

"Thank you, Sheriff." Wood took the note to the jury and asked them to pass it around so all twelve of them could see it.

"Sheriff, did you check the note for fingerprints?"

"Yes, we did."

"And whose prints did you find on it?"

"We found both Dawkins's and Tallulah Ivey's prints on it."

A few gasps could be heard in the courtroom.

"That night, Sheriff, when you questioned the defendant, did she say she was aware of a note in his hand?"

"She said she remembered seeing something in his hand, but she didn't know what it was."

"Did she say she touched the note while it was in his hand?"

"She said she had *not* touched it."

"How do you suppose her prints got on the note?"

"Objection, calls for speculation," Acuff said.

"Sustained," Judge Chapman said.

"Did you discover anything else about the note?"

"Yes, tape had been placed on the note. But it was on backwards."

"Explain what you mean by the tape being on backwards." Butch took him through the same conclusion he and I had discussed—facing out, not in.

"Did you find anything else unusual about the note?"

"We did. The letter c in the word innocence was flawed."

Wood held up a poster with a large ç in the middle for Turnbull and the jury to see. "Is this what the letter looks like?"

"Yes."

He took the note back to the jurors. "I'd like for each of you to see this for yourself. You may have missed it the first time."

He waited. Each juror nodded after they had studied it.

"Now, Sheriff, did Mr. Dawkins own a typewriter?

"Yes, he did."

"Did you check it to determine if it also had this same ç?"

"We did."

"And what did you discover?"

"His typewriter did not have the same ç."

"Did you find a typewriter that does have this flaw in the letter c?"

"Yes, at Mr. Grater's house, where the RTO folks are staying."

"Now, Sheriff, are we to understand that the note in Andrew Dawkins's hand not only had the defendant's fingerprints on it, but also had this same flawed ç?"

"That's correct."

"Where is the typewriter now?"

"We had found it in Mr. Goldsmith's room at the Grater house, but now it's gone."

"Gone? Explain, please."

"In our initial search, we were given permission by Mr. Goldsmith to have a look at the movie company's typewriters. We found one in his room. We typed the letter c and it had the same flawed key. We were then informed by Mr. Goldsmith that we'd have to leave and return with a search warrant. By the time we received the warrant and searched the house again, the typewriter was gone."

"Did you hear anyone, including Mr. Goldsmith, mention that the typewriter was shared by several members of the movie crew?"

"Yes. They had two typewriters, both shared by everybody. Oh, and there was Andy Chinn's typewriter, which he used while he boarded with Deputy McRae." Butch nodded in my direction.

"Did you check it?"

"We did. There was no flawed c."

"But let's be very clear about the two typewriters at the Grater home. Did the defendant have access to it?"

"Yes."

"Did the note have any handwriting on it?"

"No, sir. It was typed."

"So is it fair to say there's no way to determine for certain if Mr. Dawkins actually typed the note?"

"That's correct."

"Thank you, sheriff. I have no further questions."

Judge Chapman addressed Acuff. "Does the defense wish to cross-examine?"

After breaking off a private conversation with one of his team, Acuff said, "We do, Your Honor."

Acuff approached the witness stand. "Sheriff Turnbull, do you believe in coincidences?"

"What do you mean?"

"Well, for example, let's take the defendant's fingerprints

on the note that's been mentioned. Isn't it possible that the defendant reached out and touched the note while it was in Mr. Dawkins's hand? After all, she even told you that she saw something in his hand."

"I suppose it's possible, but she didn't mention touching it when I questioned her."

"But, Sheriff, she was in a state of shock. Isn't it possible, when you interviewed her in those early morning hours, she may have forgotten about touching the note?"

"She didn't appear to be in shock to me."

Acuff faced the jury. "The jury will learn from the defendant herself that she *does* remember touching the note. And Sheriff, let me ask about the typewriter with the flawed ç key. Isn't it possible that the manufacturer shipped out several typewriters with the same flawed key?"

"I don't know. I suppose it is."

"So the flawed ç could have come from any typewriter, not necessarily one owned by RTO Studios?"

"I suppose."

"And the note with the tape. Isn't it possible that Mr. Dawkins, in his haste to attach it to the window, simply put the tape on backwards?"

"I'm not sure. I suppose it's possible."

"You see, Sheriff, that's what I mean by coincidence. To convict my client, there must be no reasonable doubt she committed premeditated murder. And she did no such thing. Tallulah Ivey shot a man trying to enter her bedroom. Sheriff Turnbull, does Mississippi law allow a person to protect themselves from bodily harm?"

"Yes. But is that what—"

"No further questions, Your Honor."

Turnbull shifted in his chair and glared at Acuff.

Judge Chapman said, "Sheriff, you may be excused." Chapman looked up at the courtroom wall clock. It was twelve-thirty. "Court will be adjourned until two-thirty.

Lunch time. Butch left the courtroom still steaming over Acuff cutting him off.

Oneeda, Mary, and I ate at Charlie's Place. After we finished our sandwiches, I proposed a wager. "Who believes Tully Ivey will go to prison?"

Oneeda raised her hand.

Mary turned to Oneeda. "What makes you think that?"

"She's guilty as sin," Oneeda said.

"She might have done it," I said, "but why don't we put a little wager on whether she's going to prison, shall we? Mary and I will each bet you four dollars that she goes free. Oneeda, you'll either win eight dollars, or lose eight. Whadda you say?"

Mary nodded her agreement. Oneeda shook our hands. "Deal," she said, smiling.

We returned to the courthouse at two-fifteen.

25
My Testimony

At two thirty-five, court was back in session.

"The State of Mississippi calls Deputy Martha McRae to the stand."

Releasing my grip on Oneeda and Mary's arms, I approached the bailiff and was sworn in.

Wood walked to the witness box. I rested my hands in my lap and took a breath.

Wood asked the same questions he'd asked me during the grand jury proceeding. Especially important to him was my subsequent conversation with Ivey in her car, along with the tarot cards. I was sure he wanted the jury to know about Ivey's fascination with witchcraft.

Acuff objected along the way, but the judge overruled him each time.

Then Wood asked about *The Killing*.

Acuff objected. "Your Honor, the movie script has no relevance whatsoever. It is hearsay on hearsay. It is being used for the sole purpose to prejudice and influence the jury."

Judge Chapman didn't agree. "Overruled. I'd like to hear this."

Acuff shook his head, plopped back in his chair, and pecked his pencil on the table, loud.

I went on to explain the gist of the script, how it portrayed Mississippi in a bad light regarding Sonny Sartain's execution and capital punishment.

Finished, I glanced at the jurors to see if my testimony had any effect. Their faces were blank. Some were taking notes.

Wood placed his hand on the witness box. "I understand you were chosen as an extra in the movie. Please explain the details of that scene in which you participated."

Acuff stood. "Objection! Your Honor, this testimony is irrelevant, prejudicial, and inflammatory."

"Overruled," Chapman said. "Continue, Deputy McRae."

Me? Even I knew Wood's questions weren't relevant to this case. I figured Governor Barrett had had a chat with Judge Chapman about The Killing and wanted to make sure the jury heard it.

In detail, I explained how RTO had filmed that scene with the actor writhing in agony.

Wood asked, "What *really* happened at Sonny Sartain's execution, Mrs. McRae?"

"It was by the books. A gas chamber execution. He simply slumped over. I was there. I saw it."

"I have no further questions for this witness," Wood said, smiling.

Judge Chapman looked at Acuff. "Does the defense wish to cross-examine?" I glanced over at the defense team. Acuff was tapping his pencil on his notepad. Lightly, this time.

"Yes, Your Honor." He rose and paced toward me. "Was Tallulah Ivey involved in the movie scene you witnessed?"

"No."

"Did that scene have anything to do with the unfortunate death of Andrew Dawkins?"

"No," I repeated.

"No further questions," Acuff said, returning to his table, as he shot the judge a wicked look. But Judge Chapman was studying his watch.

Chapman tapped his gavel and adjourned court until nine-thirty the next morning.

On Wednesday morning at six o'clock the phone rang. I was barely awake.

"Martha, I'm glad I caught you," Cheri whispered. "The judge's letter finally arrived late yesterday. The sheriff wants to leave for Los Angeles on a two o'clock flight tomorrow. I shouldn't be telling you this. I could get in real trouble. Please promise you won't mention this to anyone."

"I promise. Why did it take so long to get the bank subpoena and letter from the judge?"

"All I know is that he was a new judge. When I called out

there several weeks ago to check on it for the sheriff, I was told the judge was sick and having some sort of operation."

"No wonder it took so long. And Cheri, thank you. I won't tell a soul about this."

I'd miss two and a half days of the trial, but I didn't care. I wanted to be there when the lockbox was opened. Truth be told, I was way beyond just helping Shirley get to the bottom of this. I wanted to be the first one to open that lockbox.

26
The Lockbox

That afternoon, with the trial still going on, I boarded a flight for Los Angeles. I walked down the aisle, searching ahead to make sure Butch hadn't changed plans and decided to take this flight. No sheriff. Thank goodness. He'd probably spend the night in Los Angeles tomorrow and show up at the bank on Friday.

I arrived at seven o'clock and checked into a Holiday Inn. The next morning, I took a taxi to City National's main branch. I wanted to get my bearings and know where to position myself when Butch arrived.

It was the typical main bank branch—broad columns stretching floor to ceiling, forty feet tall.

I decided where I'd sit the next day, and left.

I stayed in my room most of the day, venturing out only for lunch and supper.

When the bank opened at nine Friday morning, I was there, but not in khakis. I was wearing Tully Ivey's gift—the designer dress. No sense raising alarms at the bank by being in a deputy's uniform. Taking a seat in the lobby, I waited. I sorta felt like a rich person, wearing this designer dress and all. At ten after ten,

Butch stepped through the revolving front door. I hid behind a *Los Angeles Times*.

He marched straight to one of the manager's desks. They talked. Within five minutes, a prim looking, suit-and-tie walked over. Turnbull showed him the paperwork. They exchanged a few words and started walking in my direction. I pulled the *Times* down and stood.

"Butch, I don't want you to be mad at me. I paid for my own tick—"

"Martha! What in—what in tarnation are you doing here?" I knew he wanted to cuss me out, but was nice enough to refrain. "I should arrest you right now for obstructing justice."

"Butch, I'm not leaving, so, let's find out together what's in that lockbox. I'm invested in this as much as you are."

The bank manager asked, "Uhh, is there a problem here? Maybe I should call security."

"No, no, she's okay. Let's just get on with it." Turnbull walked towards the bank vault door. The manager didn't budge.

Turning back, Butch said, "I showed you the letter. You have the subpoena. Let's go. She can tag along. I don't care."

"Something's not right," the bank manager said. "The request for access indicates only a Sheriff Turnbull would be present."

Dropping his chin and closing his eyes, Butch said, "Martha, Martha, look what you've done. Just—just go wait in the lobby."

Turning to the manager, I said, "Please allow me to introduce myself. I'm Deputy Martha McRae. I'm one of Sheriff Turnbull's deputies. And his ex-wife." (I fibbed, of course.) "He doesn't want me here because I was the one who solved this case." I gave Butch a look of disgust he'd never forget, then faced the manager again.

"Are you married?"

"I am."

"Then you know what it's like to have a bossy wife, don't you?"

"I suppose."

"Then let us get on with our business, and we'll be out of your hair in five minutes. Are you okay with that? Because I can be a lot more bossy than this if I need to be." I don't know what came over me.

Butch stared at me like I was from another planet while the banker pondered for a few seconds.

"Well, if it's all right with Sheriff Turnbull, I suppose it's okay," he said.

"Of course it's okay with the sheriff. Right, Butch?"

"She can come," he said reluctantly, but making sure I'd never forget his peeved look.

We were escorted to the vault.

Inside, the manager used his keys to open the deposit box, then left us alone.

Butch stretched two rubber gloves over his hands and removed the lockbox, placing it on a metal table in the middle of the room. My heart beat faster than an unborn baby's. For a brief moment, we glanced at each other.

He lifted the lid and we looked inside. On top of an envelope was the Devil tarot card. It depicted a Devil sitting in a black tree, a man and a woman chained to the tree, and a snake nearby. Adam and Eve?

He reached in to retrieve it. "What's this mean?"

"Tully Ivey," I said. "She uses these cards all the time. When we get back, I'll find out what this one means."

"Well, whatever it means, it can't be good."

He placed the hideous-looking card on the table next to the box, opened the envelope, and pulled out a typewritten note.

We were close to the truth. My heart was jumping.

"I sure do hope this puts an end to this mess," Butch said.

He placed the note on the table. We bent over to read it.

Tully,

I've always admired and loved you. May God have merçy on my soul. I arranged for Rod Russell's murder. Tully, it was me. Rod Russell was a punk, a hood. I saw him beat you. He deserved to die. I know I will go to prison for this. But he deserved it.

Andrew Chinn.

"Chinn? *Andy Chinn?*" I exclaimed, astonished. "What the…?" I regained some composure and said, "Butch, Chinn uses these tarot cards, too. I saw it with my own eyes."

"I believe you."

I looked at the note again. It took me two seconds to find it. "Look, the c letter is the same ç. Right here in the word mercy."

"And Chinn had access to all the typewriters," Butch said.

"Yeah, I know. I found this same ç in a movie script he'd written. Butch, if Chinn typed both notes, what was the other one doing in Dawkins's hand?"

"We'll have to find out, won't we?" He took the edges of the Devil card along with the note and slipped them into a plastic bag.

With this new revelation staring him in the face, Butch had forgotten about my Los Angles intrusion. Thank goodness.

We landed in Memphis at five after six on Saturday morning. I felt like a busload of sleepy people had run over me.

The sheriff looked tired and beat, too. He hitched up his pants. "I'll see you at the station."

"I could use some sleep."

"Go ahead. I'll be calling Wood with this new discovery."

I changed my mind. "I don't wanna miss that."

"Suit yourself."

At station headquarters, Butch called Mike Wood. "Mr. Wood, this is Sheriff Turnbull. I just returned from California. Finally got into the lockbox. You won't believe what I found." Butch explained it all.

I was standing next to the sheriff, but couldn't hear Wood's response.

"Fine, I'll be there at three o'clock." Butch hung up. "Now, we'll just have to see what Wood does with this new evidence," he said.

"Aren't you supposed to tell Acuff about the note?"

"Nope. That's the prosecutor's job. Not mine."

At the Salem library that afternoon I found several books on tarot cards. The Devil card was my only interest. One aficionado wrote:

> There is a convincing argument that this is the most powerful and dangerous card in the deck. At its absolute worst, it is the card of the addict or the stalker, totally obsessed, enslaved, relentless. There are three essential points that a reader must make when this card appears. First, we have to be honest about our weaknesses and addictions; denial only makes it easier for them to control us. Second, it is natural to have self-interest, a desire for pleasure, and occasionally, to indulge in excesses. Doing so might even be essential to achieving our aims. This card asks us a most important question: who or what will we allow to enslave us? And who or what will be under our control? Only by understanding this part of ourselves can we gain power over it and use it to our benefit rather than letting it use us.

Rubbish. It's all a bunch of hooey.

But Chinn, leaving the Devil card for Ivey? What was he saying to her?

27
Missing Testimony

At home, I went straight to Mary's bungalow. She was sitting on her porch, sipping tea, watching Michael play on the swing set.

I was eager to know what I'd missed during the trial. "What happened in court while I was gone?"

"You best have a seat," she said. I sat beside her. "Okay, let's see… on Thursday, the day after you left, Mike Wood called Susie Parker to the stand."

"That would be logical," I said. "She'd overheard them at Charlie's Place talking about the Alamo."

"Not only did she hear them talking about that, she saw Ivey place her hand over Andrew's on the table—all intimate-like—at Charlie's Place. But Acuff cross-examined and tried to get her to say it was the movie script they were discussing. That Ivey had merely put her hand over his on top of the script."

"How'd she respond?"

"Like a champ. When Wood re-directed, Susie set the jury straight. She said the paper on the table was nothing more than napkins, not a movie script."

"Good for her! Go on, what else?"

"You know I can't remember everything. Here, you need a glass. I'll get one." She stepped into my kitchen and returned, pouring iced tea for both of us. We downed a swallow and she said, "Oh, I almost forgot… It was pure drama when Wood showed the judge and jury the restaurant receipt Susie had written that night for Andrew and Ivey's order. Susie had never been around a celebrity. She waited on them hand and foot; even remembered every item they ordered, down to refilling Ivey's water glass three times. That's when she heard Ivey mention the Alamo."

"So her testimony was credible?"

"Absolutely. Charlie even let her frame the receipt. It's on the wall at the restaurant."

"So you think she convinced the jury that Ivey and Andrew had been to the Alamo?"

"I do," Mary said.

"Yeah, movie-making certainly wasn't the only thing Dawkins and Tully Ivey had in mind, was it?"

"Oh, and you missed the funniest part. When Mike Wood asked Susie why she thought they were going to the Alamo, she said, 'Well, I don't think they went there to play patty-cake.'"

We both laughed. "Yeah, everybody laughed," Mary said. "But Judge Chapman threw that comment out."

We drank more tea.

"And get this—after she was excused, Wood called Julie Jones to the stand."

"Julie Jones? Who's that?"

"The manager from the Alamo Motel. You know, the bleach-blonde you described."

"Oh, I never knew her last name. What happened?"

"She sashayed down the aisle without a care in the world." Mary chuckled. "Ha, it was funny. When she was being sworn in, she kept smacking on gum. I couldn't believe it."

"I know all about her gum chewing. Worse than Oneeda's."

Mary rolled her eyes and continued. "Anyway, Acuff approached her and questioned how it was possible—from her reception desk—to identify Tully Ivey parked outside. But your friend, Julie, came through. She was very believable."

"She's not exactly my friend. More like a source. But at least now the jury knows they were at the Alamo. What happened next?"

"Well, Julie Jones was the last witness for the prosecution. Wood rested his case Thursday afternoon. Then, Friday morning, Acuff called Mario Mastrioni." Mary's eyes got dreamy. "I always liked him in those movies."

I waved her on, "What'd Acuff ask?"

"A bunch of garbage about how wonderful Tully Ivey was—her donations to orphanages and charities, stuff like that. Wow, did she give away a lot of money. Mastrioni said over two-hundred thousand dollars!"

"I know. I read about it when I was doing research. She's been very generous with her money."

"Yeah, but Wood objected—said character references weren't allowed in criminal court. Judge Chapman agreed, and told the clerk to strike those comments from the record."

I shifted positions in my chair, and waited for her to continue.

"Then Mastrioni talked about Ivey hugging Andrew while he was on the ground, dead. She had said, 'Oh, Andrew, what have I done?' That's when Acuff dropped a big hint on the jury. I can't remember his exact words, but this'll be close; he said, 'Well, that certainly doesn't sound like someone who'd been raped by a man. Seems to me she cared very much for Andrew Dawkins.'"

I frowned. "Mary, do you think she's innocent?"

She released a sigh. "I don't know. If someone were trying to break into my bedroom in the middle of the night I would've pulled that trigger. She could've mistaken Andrew for a stranger."

"This is like ping-pong. Back and forth, back and forth," I said.

"That's how I felt." We both took a sip of tea and she continued. "Then Acuff called Chinn to the stand. He asked him about Ivey, and how she got along with the crew."

"Yeah, he probably said she was 'trouble.'"

"No! He talked about how kind and generous she is. Said everybody enjoys working with her."

"Either he's lying on the stand, or he lied to me," I said.

"Doesn't matter. The judge threw it out just like he did Mario's testimony."

"Who else testified?"

"There were some on Friday, but I had to check on Michael. Sorry, I missed the whole day. Michael was sick."

Mary poured more tea from the pitcher. "Now, it's my turn to ask a question. What was in that lockbox?"

"You won't believe this," I said. "Another typewritten note. Guess who it's from?"

"Andrew?"

"Yes, Andrew. But not Andrew Dawkins." I grinned and stretched the suspense as long as possible. "Andrew Chinn!"

Mary's hand went to her throat. "Our Andy? The one who's staying here? Right upstairs?"

"Yes, but don't be alarmed. We're not positive he even typed the note. But get this, there was something else in the box. The Devil card."

Mary wasn't interested in hearing about any Devil card. She held a palm up and leaned in close. "Hold on, Martha. If you're saying Andy Chinn could be capable of murder," she paused to point at Michael in the back yard, "we can't stay here. It's too dangerous."

"Calm down. Butch turned the note over to the prosecution. We'll know more when the trial starts back up on Monday. If Chinn is guilty, he'll not be seeing this place again."

Mary pressed a hand to her chest and sighed. "You're sure? You're sure we're safer here than somewhere else?"

"No, I'm not a hundred percent certain. But Mary, the safest thing for us to do is sit tight until Monday."

We carried the ice tea glasses inside and started supper.

Later, Mary asked, "What'll happen to Tully Ivey's trial now that the attorneys have the note from the lockbox?"

"I don't know. We'll find out Monday morning.

PART III

New Evidence

"Will not God give justice to his elect,
who cry to him day and night?
Will he delay long over them?"

— Luke 18:7

28
Closed Doors

Nine-thirty, Monday morning, July fifteen. Court was back in session.

When the crops are green and the sun is out, the Delta humidity is so thick you can push it around with your hand, but never rid yourself of it. It sticks to you, like juice from the plants.

It was more of the same inside—people fanning their faces, wiping sweat from their arms.

Judge Chapman asked defense counsel Acuff to call his next witness. Instead, Acuff asked for permission to call Andy Chinn again.

Wood objected, "May I remind the court that the defense cannot re-direct a witness he's already redirected."

Acuff didn't hesitate. "Your Honor, yesterday I received new evidence which I believe could exonerate my client."

The judge called both attorneys to the bench. They carried on a private conversation. Surely, it was about the lockbox note.

After they broke off, the judge said, "I want to see both counselors, the sheriff, and Deputy McRae in my chambers." He tapped his gavel and the courtroom emptied—except for the four of us.

In the judge's chambers, we all stood, except Judge Chapman. He lounged in his chair and wiped sweat from his brow. A ceiling fan whirled in slow circles. I wasn't sure if it was pushing hot air out, or bringing it in from the open windows.

Chapman rubbed his eyes. "Why wasn't I apprised of this new evidence before today?"

Wood answered, "Judge, I tried to contact you yesterday, but your wife said you were working in your garden."

"Okay, okay," the judge said. "I need to hear about this new evidence before we proceed. Sheriff, why don't you read it to me."

Wood handed Butch the note and he read it. "'Tully, I've always admired and loved you. May God have mercy on my soul. I arranged for Rod Russell's murder. Tully, it was me. Rod Russell was a punk, a hood. I saw him beat you. He deserved to die. I know I will go to prison for this. But he deserved it.'" Butch paused and continued, "It's signed, Andrew Chinn. Well, it's not exactly signed." He held it up for all of us to see. "His name is typed."

The judge held out a hand and said, "Let me see it."

Acuff moved closer, and leaned over the judge's desk. "Your Honor, this is the note that came to my attention just yesterday. It appears we have a new wrinkle in the case. This new evidence can prove my client's innocence. In fact, if anyone should be on trial, it should be Andy Chinn for murdering Rod Russell. His note is a confession. My client was just defending herself from an intruder."

"It's typed. How can we be sure it's from Andy Chinn?" Wood asked the judge.

"Still, Your Honor," Acuff said, "it's evidence that should be permitted."

The judge turned to Butch. "Is this your theory, Sheriff? You think Andy Chinn typed both notes, and one of them contains his confession in this Russell murder?"

"It seems that way, Your Honor. It's my theory that Chinn had a—a, whadda you call it, Martha?"

"A delusional attachment," I said, "meaning he loved her and thought she loved him."

Acuff was quick to say, "So now, Your Honor, we have Chinn in the middle of all this. It's possible he'd been at the Grater house late that night, taped the note on the window, was leaving, but saw Dawkins go to the window and get shot. That's when he changed his mind and decided not to confess to the Russell murder. He was probably trying to retrieve the note from the lockbox when he was caught in Los Angeles."

"I don't see it that way, Judge," Wood argued. "Chinn doesn't come across as delusional. Tully Ivey knew what was happening. She was involved. She's complicit, and I intend to prove it."

Acuff stepped closer to Judge Chapman. "Your Honor, let the jury determine if this lockbox note—this new evidence—exonerates my client. I'm imploring you to allow it."

Judge Chapman sighed and asked, "Sheriff, do you have any other evidence this court is not aware of?"

"Nothing your honor."

Wood stepped forward and placed a finger on the edge of Chapman's desk. "We don't understand what this note means, Your Honor. We still don't have proof that Chinn typed either of the notes, or even put one in the lockbox. There's no signature. It could have been placed there by anyone. Even Goldsmith. Your Honor, I believe it's too early to allow it. It will only confuse the jury."

"Maybe you're right," Chapman said with a sigh. He rubbed his chin in thought for a minute, then turned his chair around to look out the window. Nobody moved a muscle while the judge cogitated.

He turned to face us. "I've made my decision. The note will not be allowed as evidence at this time, and it is not to be discussed with anyone—no one. Not until we determine what it means. I'm willing to change my mind later during this trial, but not just yet. Do all of you understand?"

Everyone nodded. Even a reluctant Acuff.

"And Counselor Acuff," the judge said, drying his forehead, "you may call Chinn back to the stand, but you better not mention this lockbox note. Understood?"

Acuff nodded.

Judge Chapman looked at the wall clock in his office. "It's ten-thirty. I'll call for a recess until one-thirty. That's all."

Mary had waited for me in the hallway. She wanted to know everything about the private meeting in the judge's chambers. I told her none of us were allowed to discuss it. She respected that. We returned to the courthouse at one-fifteen, where Oneeda joined us.

We found Shirley Dawkins and practically forced her to sit with us. We knew she was going through a lot, what with Andrew's indiscretion and all. Mary sat beside her and held her hand. This was the same Mary who thought Andrew was going to marry *her*!

Later, I used my print shop to make a plaque for Mary. It fit her to a tee.

"All rise," the bailiff bellowed.

Judge Chapman sat and addressed Acuff. "Defense counsel may call its next witness."

Once again, Acuff called Chinn.

My thoughts? Acuff better tiptoe through his questions if he's going to obey the judge's order about not revealing the lockbox note.

“Mr. Chinn, there are just a few things I’d like to clear up,” Acuff said.

Chinn’s face tightened.

“Let’s go back to the night of August tenth, last year. Tell the court where you were that night.”

“I told you, Martha McRae’s boarding house.”

“Actually, you were outside Tully Ivey’s window, weren’t you? Remember, you’re under oath, Mr. Chinn.”

Judge Chapman leaned forward, staring at Acuff like a mama who’d caught her little boy about to reach in the cookie jar.

“I—I don’t know what you’re talking about.” Chinn said, shifting positions in the witness chair. He blinked rapidly and searched the courtroom, like he was looking for someone to help him.

“Mr. Chinn, the note in Mr. Dawkins’s hand mentioned a lockbox and a key on the ledge. Do you have the missing lockbox key in your possession, maybe hidden away somewhere?”

Chinn’s eyelids flew open. “No, absolutely not. Are you insinuating I had something to do with Mr. Dawkins’s death? This is ridiculous!”

Acuff casually stretched his arm over the side of the witness stand and looked out at the packed courtroom. “No, Mr. Chinn, I wasn’t insinuating anything. I was just asking if you had the key.” Acuff gave the judge another look of irritation—likely still frustrated Chapman hadn’t allowed the lockbox contents as evidence.

Acuff wasn't finished. "In your earlier testimony, Mr. Chinn, you said this about Tallulah Ivey, and I quote, 'She gets along with everybody. People love working with her. She's giving, compassionate. I'd say she's loved by everybody. She'd give you the shirt off her back if you asked her.' End quote."

Acuff smiled for the first time in a long time. 'Now, Mr. Chinn, I'm not sure that last part is an appropriate analogy, but we get your point—she's generous."

Wood objected. "Your honor, this testimony has already been stricken from the record."

The judge leaned back and rubbed his jaw. "Overruled. I'm going to allow it this time."

I suppose the judge wanted to hear more, but wasn't ready to reveal the note to the jury.

"Defense may continue," Chapman said.

"Thank you, Your Honor." Acuff turned to his witness. "Mr. Chinn, I have here Deputy McRae's notes from her interview with you on September twenty-fourth, last year. These are your words. 'I just stay out of her way. Always thought she was trouble. Let's just say she could absorb anyone she wanted. She owned you. The men who were close to her became like putty in her hands, doing whatever she wanted.' End quote. So, which is it, Mr. Chinn—is she trouble, or is she loved by everybody?"

Chinn brushed make-believe lint off his trousers, nervous-like. "Maybe I said those things to make her seem like a bad person."

"Why would you do that?"

Chinn looked down. "I don't know. I—I suppose I was angry with her at the time."

"Why were you angry with her?"

He shifted in his chair. "The men. All the men she was involved with."

"So you were jealous?"

"Maybe."

"Maybe? I'll take that as a yes. How long have you been jealous of Mrs. Ivey?"

"I never said I was."

"Mr. Chinn, why don't you go ahead and confess that you taped that note on Tully Ivey's window and encouraged Mr. Dawkins to pay a visit to Tallulah Ivey's bedroom that night, knowing she had been traumatized before and would likely shoot him? You did that, didn't you?"

"No, I had nothing to do with it."

Acuff stared at him and shook his head.

"I have no more questions of this witness.

My theory? Chinn typed the notes and planned the whole thing. And he must've had Rod Russell murdered.

Yet, something was still amiss. Like the key, and the answer to why the note was in Dawkins's hand to begin with.

"Mr. Wood, does the State of Mississippi wish to cross-examine?" Chapman asked.

"Not at this time, Your Honor."

Acuff called Banner O'Brien to the stand.

"Mr. O'Brien, how long have you known Tully Ivey?"

"Approximately eleven years."

"In how many movies have you directed her?"

"Nine."

"Have you ever seen her angry?"

"No. She's always acted in a professional manner. Like the others have said, everybody enjoyed working with her. Just being around her was invigorating."

"How do you explain what Andrew Chinn said about her?"

O'Brien shrugged. "I can't. I suppose he loved her."

"Had you ever noticed Andy Chinn's affection for her?"

"No, I can't say I have."

"Did she ever mention to you why she wanted to own a pistol?"

O'Brien fidgeted. "Yes. After the restraining order on Rod Russell in Los Angeles, she told me she had purchased a .38 revolver. She said she felt safer having it around."

"And to your knowledge, did she have any kind of relationship with Mr. Dawkins, other than in their respective roles in the movie?"

"If she knew him outside of filming, I didn't know it."

Acuff rubbed his chin. "Were you there that night, August tenth?"

"I was."

"When you saw Tallulah Ivey outside, would you say she was upset?"

"She was crying," O'Brien said. "For heaven's sake, she'd just shot a man. Of course she was upset." With an excited voice, he added, "She didn't intend to kill that man. She thought he was an intruder."

"Is that what she told you? Did she think Mr. Dawkins was an intruder?"

"Yes."

"But she must've known him. She was down on the ground and said, 'Oh, Andrew, what have I done?' What did you say to the other RTO men standing around, watching that?"

"I can't remember what I said."

"Oh? Well, allow me to refresh your memory." Acuff flipped some pages in his notes. "According to Sheriff Turnbull's testimony, you said, 'She must've liked him an awful lot.' Isn't that what you said?"

"I guess so. I'd forgotten."

Acuff marched to the jury box. "You know, Mr. O'Brien, I keep wondering why a woman who cared so much about a man would shoot him in cold blood."

Wood bolted up. "Your Honor, is that a question defense counsel is asking, or is it his attempt to prejudice the jury with his suppositions?"

"Sustained." Judge Chapman instructed the jurors to disregard Acuff's last statement and had it stricken from the records.

"I have no further questions, Your Honor," Acuff said, taking a seat. He seemed to be pleased. Maybe he had just injected more doubt in the jurors' minds.

Chapman looked at Wood, "Does the State wish to cross-examine?"

"Yes, Your Honor." Wood approached O'Brien.

"Mr. O'Brien, have you ever had an intimate relationship with Mrs. Tallulah Ivey?"

O'Brien squirmed in his chair and hesitated to answer.

Suddenly, Wood held up several eight-by-ten photographs, waving them in the air so vigorously nobody could focus on the images. "I remind you, you're under oath, and I'm sure you're aware of the penalty for perjury."

O'Brien's eyes followed the photos. "Well, most of us at RTO—you know—kinda knew her in that way."

Whispers filled the courtroom.

Wood returned to his table and placed the photographs face down.

Those probably weren't even some sleazy, private detective photographs of her with O'Brien. Wood had bluffed.

He approached O'Brien again. "So Tallulah Ivey had intimate relations with lots of RTO men," he said. "That being the case, what makes you so confident Mrs. Ivey had some *special* feeling for Andrew Dawkins?"

"Objection," Acuff said. "This entire line of questioning is irrelevant."

"Overruled," Chapman said. "You may answer the question, Mr. O'Brien."

"To tell you the truth, I don't know. Mr. Acuff and I discussed this point."

I looked over at Acuff. He was tapping his pencil hard on a legal pad.

"And when did you and Mr. Acuff discuss this?"

"When we rehearsed my testimony."

"Oh, really? You rehearsed your testimony with Mr. Acuff? Well, my goodness."

"He said it was necessary."

"I'm sure he did." Wood looked towards the jury, shook his head and pursed his lips.

Even I knew witnesses were coached to some extent before a trial. But the jury probably didn't know that.

Wood was trying to discredit O'Brien's testimony.

"I have no more questions for this witness," Wood said.

It was four-thirty, so Judge Chapman tapped his gavel. “This court is adjourned until nine thirty tomorrow morning.”

Mary and I left the courthouse for an early supper at Charlie’s Place.

Charlie strolled over, wiping his palms on a barbeque-stained apron. “So ladies, seems like we’re always havin’ some sort o’ scandal in the Delta, don’t it?”

We smiled.

“Evil has a way of finding us,” I said.

“Oh, it’s the devil, all right,” Charlie said. “I know, ’cause these Hollywood fellas been coming in from day one, playing with those fortune cards.”

I perked up. “They’re tarot cards. Did you hear anything?”

“Matter o’ fact, I might’ve. Some weeks ago, I heard two of ’em talking in that booth right over there.” He pointed over my shoulder. “I heard this one fella talking about how they’d never find it. He said, ‘It’s at the bottom of the river.’ Then he flipped over one o’ those cards and they both laughed.”

I was stunned by this new information. “Why didn’t you go to the police and tell ’em what you heard?”

“What those men said meant nothin’ to me. My mind was fixated on those cards.”

“Charlie, if I come back in the morning will you look at some photographs?” I was eager to know if one of the men Charlie overheard was staying out at the Grater house.

"Sure. Of course," he said.

I'd miss more testimony the next day; but what Charlie Parker might provide could be more important.

Later that night, I retrieved file photos of the crew from my *Gazette* office.

At nine the next morning, I walked into Charlie's Place with a file folder of photographs. We sat in a booth. I presented photos of each crew member.

"Nope, that's not the one . . . Nope, not him. . . Him, either."

I placed Chinn's photograph on the table.

"That's him."

I was getting closer and closer to Freddie's murderer—Andy Chinn. But why? Why him?

It was noon, so I headed to the café for lunch. Mary was waiting for me. At some point I knew I'd need to fill her in on what I'd learned from Charlie about Chinn being a possible murderer. Just not right away. First, I wanted to know who had testified that morning.

I sat in a booth opposite her. "What'd I miss?"

"Let's see… oh, Al Goldsmith testified. You should have seen him. He strutted to the stand with a big ol' smug frown on his face."

"I know the look. Who was questioning him? Acuff?"

"Yep. He asked him about Ivey's charity donations, but Wood objected and it wasn't allowed. After that, Acuff didn't ask much else. But Wood sure did cross-examine him about *The Killing*. He wanted Goldsmith to bring up capital punishment. I think Wood wanted him to say how evil we are for allowing it."

"That's exactly what the movie is intended to show," I said.

"Yeah, but Goldsmith was sneaky. He didn't talk about capital punishment. He lied and said the movie was about the Delta. About us. What outstanding citizens we are. Stuff like that."

"What'd Wood do?"

"You woulda loved this part." Mary leaned forward. "He took the script and read the scene where Ivey plays a reporter and tells one of her New York friends what barbarians we are."

"Do you remember the scene?"

"Mmm, sorry, I can't remember what she said."

"Well, I just happen to have the script right here in my purse. Let's find the scene. I marked that scene for the governor. It shouldn't be hard to find."

We began thumbing through the pages and soon found it.

"Here it is," I said. "This sums up the whole movie. Tully Ivey is playing the part of a reporter who witnessed the execution of Sonny Sartain. She's explaining to her friend what she saw."

I asked Mary to read the scene. She did her best to mimic Tully Ivey. "'It was awful, I tell you. They strapped him to a chair in a chamber and released poisonous gas. The man went into convulsions, banging his head on some pole behind his head. His eyes almost popped out of his head. He drooled from his mouth—all while the holier than thou witnesses watched. It was awful,

I tell you. It was barbaric.'"

"Finally, the jury knows what the movie is really about." Made me feel sorta proud. "Did you see how the jury reacted?"

"They glared at Goldsmith like he was the Devil himself."

"Good."

"Oh, and Judge Chapman is ill. There's no more testimony this afternoon," Mary said.

I drank some water to clear my throat. "Mary, I don't want you getting upset when I tell you this, but it's only fair you should know."

She perked up. "Only fair I know what? Is this about Andy?"

"Yes. I believe he had something to do with Freddie's murder."

"Martha, we need to move out. Now. Or you should throw *him* out!"

"Then he'd know *we know*. It's safer if we just stay put and act normal."

"But Michael. He could be in danger."

"It'd be more dangerous if Chinn thought we knew. I'm explaining all this to Butch tomorrow. He'll make sure we're protected."

29

The Diva's Testimony

The next morning, Judge Chapman sneezed, blew his nose, and told the defense to call their next witness.

Frank Acuff stood and announced, "The defense calls Tallulah Ivey."

The courtroom erupted into a beehive of whispers and rustling bodies. We had waited days for this moment.

When she stepped from behind the defense table and strode to the witness box, it was if the entire courtroom belonged to her. She looked regal, dressed in all white, with a Princess of Monaco hair bun and white bow. She looked as innocent as a lamb. I'd seen her look like this in a movie—the title I couldn't recall.

Oneeda whispered in my ear, "The Last Princess, 1949."

That was it.

Acuff approached her, smiling.

"Mrs. Ivey—may I call you Mrs. Ivey? Or would you prefer Miss Ivey?"

"Miss Ivey, if you don't mind," she said in eloquent Southern dialect.

"Now, Miss Ivey, this courtroom has heard a lot of people talk about you during this trial, but now we have a chance to hear what the most important person in this courtroom has to say. You. You alone know what happened that unfortunate night."

She never allowed her gaze to escape Acuff as he paced the floor between her and the jury.

"Miss Ivey, I've learned over the years that the jury is always interested in a defendant's background, in their upbringing. Tell us about your childhood, what it was like. For instance, you grew up in an orphanage, is that right?"

"Yes."

She told a long, sad tale of her childhood—abandoned by her parents, taken to an orphanage; how the nuns had pushed her to perform because they saw her natural beauty; and finally, God's will for her life in the movies. She had the jury and the courtroom mesmerized. It was an Oscar-winning performance. But she never said a word about any abuse from a priest.

Then Acuff surprised me and everyone to no end.

"Tallulah Ivey, did you have intimate relations with Andrew Dawkins at the Alamo Motel on August three, 1962?"

"I did. I'm sorry, but yes, I did."

I was in shock. Why had Acuff changed his tactic about her relationship with Dawkins?

She lowered her head and used a handkerchief to wipe a tear. "I know I denied it before and I'm sorry for that. But I really did like him. Maybe even loved him. He was so kind and gentle. Not like most of the men in my life."

What a lie.

Acuff leaned against the witness box. "Tell this court why you had earlier denied having this tryst with him."

"Honestly, I thought it would reflect poorly on me, since I had to shoot him and all," she said, facing the jury. "I thought he was an intruder breaking in to hurt me. I didn't shoot him on purpose." She dabbed away more tears.

"Thank you, I believe the jury has heard enough," Acuff said, easing into his chair behind the defense table. "No more questions, Your Honor."

Wood approached for his cross-examination with an ah shucks attitude. He stood beside Ivey at the witness stand, hands in his pockets, gazing out over the courtroom.

"Mrs. Ivey, tell the court approximately how many men you've intimately known in your lifetime."

"Objection. Irrelevant and inflammatory," Acuff said.

Wood piped up. "Your Honor, the defense's own witness left an opening for this line of questioning. I simply intend to pursue it."

"Overruled," the judge said to Acuff. "Answer the question, Mrs. Ivey."

"It's impossible to know," she said without batting an eye.

"Well, Mrs. Ivey, Mr. Chinn has testified that you had intimate relations with many of the men at RTO Studios. Is his statement true?"

"Of course it's true."

"Which ones? Which men in this courtroom might he be referring to?"

She looked around the courtroom, searching. "Well, let's see… there's Andrew Chinn… and Banner… but not Randall or Alston," she looked at each of them in succession, "and let's see now, whom am I missing? Yes, there he is—Mario," she said, smiling at him. "Well, I can't seem to find any others here today."

Wood put a fist to his mouth and faked a cough, then grinned. "Mrs. Ivey, we all know the Hollywood lifestyle is, shall we say, more liberal than what we know in the South, but what I'm getting at is this—why would Andrew Dawkins come to your window at midnight? Isn't it because you invited him there? You had planned on shooting him, hadn't you? I'm guessing those tarot cards you use to predict the future—"

"Objection, Your Honor," Acuff said, scowling. "Which question would the prosecution like for the defendant to answer first? He has asked so many."

Mister Acuff," Ivey said, holding her hand up to halt her own attorney's objection. "It doesn't bother me that he's asking these questions." She faced Wood and said, "The answer to your question, Mr. Wood, is that I didn't invite Andrew to my window that night. Not that night, not ever. I had nothing to do with those notes, and I certainly didn't murder Andrew Dawkins."

Wood conferred with his colleagues, and returned to the witness stand. "How long have you owned the .38 revolver used to shoot Mr. Dawkins?"

“Five years, I suppose.”

“Did you have firearms training?”

“Of course. In California. I’m licensed to carry a weapon.”

“Why would you own a weapon?”

“For my safety. I would never allow a man to take advantage of me.”

“What do you mean ‘take advantage’ of you?”

“Don’t you know? Oh, I forgot, you’re a man. You wouldn’t understand,” she said, smiling towards the jury.

“In your firearms training did the instructor teach you about ‘rules of engagement’? In other words, were you taught the circumstances under which it is lawful to use deadly force against another human being?”

She raised her head even higher. “I was taught to fire at anyone trying to enter my bedroom.”

Wood seemed agitated, not able to get the upper hand.

“How many times have you been married?”

“Objection,” Acuff said. “The prosecution continues to ask these non-relevant, inflammatory questions.”

“Overruled. I’ll allow the question,” Chapman said.

Wood thanked the judge and faced Ivey again. “How many times?”

“Oh, I don’t mind answering the question,” she said, looking up at the judge. “Three times. Each man was the most beautiful creature I'd ever met. But you know what they say—a woman is never complete until she's married. Then she's finished."

Cackles permeated the courtroom. I didn't know whether to laugh or cry at the absurd lack of moral character in this woman.

She wasn't finished. "Mr. Wood, most bad marriages end in a slow leak. All mine ended in blowouts. Ill-advised marriages, you might say."

Wood ignored her comment. He walked to his table and conferred with his assistants again.

He seemed frustrated by his inability to rattle her. Me? I hoped the jury would see through her charade. Most of them had slack mouths, like they'd been gazing upon a goddess. A goddess with no morals.

When Wood declared he had no more questions, Judge Chapman called for a lunch recess.

At two forty-five, a fully-engaged sun aimed its energy directly into the Greenlee Courthouse. I was born with a sensitive nose, and the perspiration in the packed courtroom was unmistakable. Even Judge Chapman stretched out his bow tie, releasing the chokehold of this collar.

Acuff stood and asked for a redirect of Tully Ivey. The judge signified his approval with a weary, "You may."

"Miss Ivey, I'm going to ask you a very direct, very pointed question," Acuff said. "Did you willfully and knowingly shoot Andrew Dawkins on the night of August ten, 1962?"

"No, of course not. I had no idea the intruder was someone I actually knew." Her eyes and face telegraphed a convincing innocence only a trained actor could master. She also was the only person in the courtroom not sweating. I wanted to investigate what make-up miracle she'd discovered.

"Again, tell the jury how well you knew Mr. Dawkins," Acuff said.

"Banner O'Brien chose him for a part in the movie," she said. "Yes, we did go to dinner the night it rained. And yes, we did go to the Alamo Motel. And well, you know where I'm going with this."

"I do. Now, Miss Ivey, the prosecution has brought up those tarot cards you play with. He claims they're some sort of witchcraft. But in fact, are they not simply mild entertainment for—"

Oneeda—sitting right beside me!—jumped to her feet and yelled, "They're evil sorcery, forbidden by God!"

Chapman tapped his gavel and pointed it at Oneeda. "Lady, I'll place you in contempt of court if you disrupt my courtroom one more time."

Her outburst startled me, but didn't surprise me. At some point in her life, Oneeda must've had a filterectomy, where the filter between her brain and mouth had been removed.

When the courtroom returned to order, Acuff inquired again, "Are the tarot cards just entertainment for you?"

"Yes, entertainment."

Acuff had no more questions and excused her.

"The defense may call its next witness," Chapman said.

Acuff said, "Your Honor, the defense rests."

Judge Chapman announced, "Closing arguments will be heard next Monday, nine-thirty a.m."

"All rise," the bailiff shouted. Judge Chapman and his flowing robes exited the courtroom.

I met Butch in the hallway. "Where can we talk, privately?"

He pulled me aside. "Tell me now."

"Charlie Parker has identified Andy Chinn as a possible suspect in Freddie's murder."

"Really?" he said, twisting around to make sure no one could hear us. "How does Charlie know?"

I explained what Charlie had overheard, and his recognition of Chinn's photograph.

"Okay, good. That's not enough to arrest him on, though. Let's sit tight until we can get proof."

We were eating supper—Mary, little Michael, Father Compañero, and I.

I'd been going on and on about the trial when Oneeda charged through the front door. "Martha!" she yelled.

"We're in the kitchen. Come on back."

She staggered through my swinging kitchen door and stopped, her hands propped against her hips. Strapped around her forehead and draped over her nose was a male athletic supporter. I almost fell out of my chair.

"O n e e d a," I said, dragging it out. "What in the world have you been doing?"

She ripped the athletic supporter off like a flamenco dancer, tossed it toward the trash can, and plopped down in a kitchen chair to join us.

"Why I've been s'plainin' to Charlie Parker and his customers what that McAllister kid did to that Lungren boyyy. They didn't believe me. Soooo one of those high school boys was there and pulled this outta his bag and wellll, here it is." She patted her head. "Ooops, nooo. There it is!" She pointed a limp finger toward the floor.

"You've been drinking," Mary said.

Oneeda tried to squeeze her thumb and index finger together. "Maybe a lit'll bit."

Mary frowned and excused herself. "I think it's time to take Michael to bed."

Father Paul's mouth was still open.

I'll admit, in the Delta, we enjoy our libations. But this was a bit much.

Oneeda was my friend, so I took care of her. Coffee and Mary's cornbread seemed to soak up most of the damage.

I took her home and convinced her to sleep in, knowing she'd never survive the next day's courtroom heat.

Later, I cleaned the kitchen by myself, which didn't make me so happy. I was bushed. I returned to my thinking spot, the kitchen table, and tried to figure out what I could do next.

The front door opened. I heard someone bound up the stairs. Andy Chinn. Had to be. I prayed that God would keep us safe. I poured a cup of Oneeda's "sober-coffee" and returned to my thoughts.

I knew the procedure. First, study what you know. Second, figure out what's missing.

I thought about the subpoena. It got us in the lockbox. But the key was still missing. If I could somehow figure out which one of the movie crew had the key, it might solve this whole sordid mess. Who had it?

Half an hour later, a decent idea came to me—I could write an article that would draw out the key-holder.

Naww, that'd never work. Would it?

It was one in the morning. I was a marshmallow. My pillow was a welcome sight.

30
The Typewriter

News came to the sheriff's office—Ivey planned to head back to Los Angeles for a long weekend. I decided to hold off writing a story about the missing key. Instead, I would pay a visit to Tully Ivey before she left town.

No one had told me that questioning a defendant during an active trial was off limits. I rushed out to the Grater house, hoping to catch her before she left. I wanted to confront her with a question that hadn't been asked during the trial—what was her relationship with Giamano Pileggi? If she gets off for Dawkins's death, maybe I can get her on Rod Russell's murder. I couldn't get Joanna Whitfield's story off my mind about the Morgan's manager seeing Ivey with Russell on the night he was murdered.

For leverage, I brought the tabloid photo of Ivey with Pileggi at Romano's restaurant. I would ask her about it.

When I arrived at the Grater house, her driver was loading luggage in a car trunk. "Excuse me, are you taking Mrs. Ivey to the airport?"

The elderly man lifted the last piece of luggage and said, "Yes'm, matter o' fact, I am."

I noticed the case in his hand. It was black, about twenty inches wide, ten inches thick. Was this the same one from

Goldsmith's desk?

"Oh, that is such a beautiful case. What's in it?"

"Not sure," he said. "I just load the luggage and drive her."

"It's alligator hide, isn't it? I study fine cases like this. May I feel the texture? Would you mind?" I reached into the trunk to pop the latches.

He gently stopped my hand. "Ma'am, I'm not sure that's a good idea to be foolin' with the Miss's things."

"Oh, but please open it for me. I won't touch it, I promise. I'd just like to see if it has that soft black velvet on the inside. Please."

He looked around to make sure nobody was watching, snapped open the latches and lifted the top, smiling. Bless his heart, he was proud to show it.

There it was. The typewriter. He carefully closed and secured the latches, surely not realizing the significance of what he'd shown me.

Tully Ivey came bustling out the front door with "puppy-dog" Carr on her heels. She was giving him a list of verbal instructions, but stopped short when she saw me.

"Now, now, Deputy McRae, whatever in the world are you doing with my luggage?"

"I was admiring the leather case."

"It's not leather, my dear. It's imitation, and you know it."

The driver closed the trunk. I stepped back as Ivey slid in the back seat, exhibiting the most steely-eyed, evil look she'd ever given me.

I pushed the tabloid photo of her with Pileggi through the window.

"Come on now, ma'am, we all know you and Giamano Pileggi were friends. Why don't you admit you had him murder Rod Russell?"

She batted my hand away so hard her diamond ring drew blood from my thumb.

I wrapped my thumb in a handkerchief and watched them drive away. A thought hit me front and center. I scrambled to my car and headed for Solo, breaking the speed limit the whole way—I had no choice. Arriving at Shirley Dawkins's house, I rushed in, not even bothering to knock, and yelled, "I need to borrow Andrew's typewriter."

"Whatever in the world for?"

"Sorry, don't have time to tell you right now," I said, rushing past her and out the back door to Andrew's office.

Finding the case in his back office, I closed it and headed for my car. "Gotta get to the airport."

"The Memphis airport?"

"Yes. And I promise to bring back a typewriter that's much more valuable," I yelled and peeled out from her gravel drive, hoping I'd arrive at the Delta terminal ahead of Ivey's chauffeur.

Three hours later, I pulled into short-term parking across from the only skycap in sight. I breathed a sigh of relief. No black sedan was in the terminal.

I retrieved a ten-dollar bill from my purse, grabbed the typewriter case, and hustled straight to the skycap.

"I'm Deputy McRae." I showed him my badge, then pressed the ten-dollar bill in his hand. "This is for helping me catch a murderer. Do you understand?"

"Ma'am, I got no idea what you talkin' 'bout." He held the bill out like it wasn't his yet.

"See this case? A woman in a black sedan will be arriving any minute. I need for you to switch this case with the one her driver hands you. Her case looks just like this one. Got it? Can you do that for me?"

"Yes'm. But what if they goes inside to the ticket counter?"

"My money's on her wanting to check her luggage out here, with you. Keep this case behind the counter. After they go inside, put this one on the conveyor belt and leave hers under the counter." I pointed toward the parking lot. "I'll be over there, watching. I'll come back for the case. Okay? You can do this, right?"

"I sure can, yes'm," he said, stuffing the ten-dollar bill in his pocket.

I retreated to my car.

When the sedan pulled to a stop, the driver opened Ivey's door, then the trunk. I couldn't hear what she said, but she motioned toward the terminal doors. I groaned. Dealing with a ticket agent would be tricky.

The skycap took a firm stance in front of the luggage, said something to them, and carried their luggage behind his counter. Ivey shrugged her shoulders, handed him some money, and went inside. The driver slid in his car and pulled away. I ran to the skycap.

"Good job," I said. "They were going to check the luggage inside. How'd you change her mind?"

"I just told 'em the ticket lady inside don't know nothin' 'bout taggin' no luggage. Most likely get lost and end up in Timbuktu—or worse, Cincinnati. Best let me handle this out here. That's what I told 'em."

"You're a genius. Thank you." I started to leave, but stopped. "By the way, what's wrong with Cincinnati?"

"My ex lives there."

Arriving home, I opened the case, rolled in some paper, and typed the letter c several times. I was relieved to see the ç. I kept typing it, grinning as I pushed the c key.

Then I phoned the Sheriff to tell him what I'd found, but he wasn't in the office. I figured Mike Wood needed to know so I called him and explained it all.

There was disappointment in his voice. "The search warrant expired long ago. Your evidence is not admissible in court. Besides, the trial's almost over."

"No. No. There has to be a way for the jury to know about this. For heaven's sake, Ivey typed both of those notes. She planned the whole thing. Don't you see?"

"Of course I do. But we're dealing with the judicial system here."

"Then get a re-trial. Bring this evidence to a new jury."

"Deputy McRae, it's up to the jury now. Monday is closing arguments. We can't re-open the case."

"Can't you present the note during closing arguments?"

"I told you, it's not allowed. Look, I want to see her convicted as much as you. I still have a chance to convince the jury. I haven't given up."

I took the typewriter to Butch. He wasn't pleased—me seizing it without a proper search warrant and all. He put it in lock-up. "Just in case," he said.

Four days later—long after each attorney had rehashed the case in their closing arguments—Mary, Oneeda, and I were rocking on Mary's porch, drinking tea, watching Michael play with his pals in the backyard.

The phone rang. I rushed in to hear Butch say that a decision from the jury had been reached. I had a bad feeling about it. Wood's case was weak at best, and the only thing we could hope for was that the truth about the movie would slap the star-struck jurors awake. If they were riled enough about being called barbaric ignorants, they might vote guilty.

But would the Mississippi men and women who had Tully Ivey's fate in their hands convict her just to protect our state's reputation? If I were a juror determining a person's guilt or innocence in a murder trial would I let something like a bad movie about my home state determine my vote? Probably not.

"All rise."

Judge Chapman sat and asked, "Has the jury reached a verdict?"

The foreman stood. "We have, Your Honor."

"Please read the verdict."

"We, the jury, find the defendant *not guilty*."

My heart sank.

Acuff and his team hugged each other. With a casual smile, Tully Ivey seemed pleased to play her role in the victor's ritual. She was free as a bird.

I sulked for a week. The filming went back into production, and nothing would ever be the same.

Mary took little Michael to Phillipsburg and moved in with an old friend. I couldn't blame her. I prayed she'd return after this mess blew over—after Chin was put away.

Oneeda and I were sipping sherry the next night, discussing Mary's departure and the actress's Oscar-winning courtroom performance.

Oneeda asked, "When did you realize she was guilty? When you switched the typewriters?"

"Yes. But I *suspected* it was her when she was on the witness stand, talking about all the men she'd known. When she came to Andy Chinn, she called him 'Andrew.' Ever notice how she always calls people by their proper names? Like Randall Carr, instead of Randy. And Alston, instead of Al. We all thought the 'Andrew' in the first note was Andrew Dawkins. I think she typed 'Andrew' on the note, not even contemplating Andrew Dawkins would be the one to show up that night. I know it's far-fetched, but it could be true. Why else would she cry over Dawkins's body? She shot the wrong man."

I took a sip of sherry and continued. "I think she set the whole lockbox charade up before she even set foot in Mississippi. She invited Andy Chinn to her bedroom that night. To shoot him."

"But why? I don't understand," Oneeda said.

"Think about it. If Tully Ivey had pulled it off, Chinn would be dead, unable to refute the lockbox note. Remember what the note said?"

"Yeah, Chinn confessed to killing that Russell fella."

"Exactly. But Chinn didn't murder Russell. Ivey did. After she got Chinn out of the picture, she probably would've had Randy Carr take the note to the tabloids and threaten a libel suit if they kept printing innuendos about her involvement in Russell's murder. She even told me those tabloid stories were hurting her career."

"But why was Andrew at her window?"

"He was just in the wrong place at the wrong time."

"So, she gets off scot-free," Oneeda said, shaking her head.

"Maybe not. Justice hasn't served her last course."

"What do you mean?"

"I mean I'm working on a plan."

"When will you tell the sheriff all this?"

"I'm not sure. It's still a theory."

"What about Freddie's murder? What does it have to do with any of this?"

"Remember Charlie Parker telling us about the two men he overheard? They talked about throwing something in the river."

"I do," she said.

"I went back and showed Charlie Parker photos of the crew. He identified Chinn. I think he killed Freddie and threw the murder weapon in the river." I felt the slump in my shoulders. "Oh, but Oneeda, I feel awful about Freddie. I shouldn't have involved him in the first place."

"Nonsense. You couldn't have known something like that would happen. You need to get over it, Martha."

"It's not easy. And now Mary's gone."

"I know. But it's time to figure out what to do next," she said.

"Next?"

"Yes, *think*, Martha. What can we do to catch him? To catch Chinn."

"You're right." Adrenaline kicked in and revived my determination. "We have to find enough evidence to get Chinn convicted for murdering Freddie. Then, we need to gather enough evidence to convict Ivey in the Russell murder."

"Goodness. But how?"

"I don't know. Not yet."

I stopped with the sherry and made coffee. "I need to think. Let's move to the kitchen. We need to write a plan of attack."

"Let's do it," she said, slapping her thigh.

Two hours later, Oneeda was asleep, her head resting peacefully in the folds of her arms on the table, while I had two pages of neatly typed notes. The plan was ready.

THE ACTRESS

PART IV

The Rest of The Story

"In him we have redemption
through his blood, the forgiveness
of our trespasses, according to
the riches of his grace, which he
lavished upon us, in all wisdom
and insight making known to us
the mystery of his will."

— Ephesians 1:7-9

31
The Plan

First on my list was Freddie's murder.

All post offices are required to have the same materials and equipment. Greenlee was no exception. I spent an hour going through every nook and cranny, searching, trying to figure out what wasn't there, but should have been—the murder weapon.

I was ready to give up.

Thirsty, I filled a paper cup at the sink. That's when I realized what was missing—Freddie's teakettle. He'd always kept it beside the sink on a hotplate. The hotplate was there, but no teakettle. The killer must've come into the post office, confronted Freddie, knocked him down and looked for something to hit him with—the teakettle. He buried the body and threw the murder weapon in the river. That was my theory.

I questioned the postmaster about it. He confirmed that there had indeed been a teakettle on the hotplate. I drove back to the river where Freddie's body was found. I searched along the river bank hoping to find a teakettle that could've washed ashore. After fifty yards or so, I encountered dead trees and limbs piled along the river's edge, halting any further search.

Most likely floated downstream, anyway. I gave up and returned to my car.

Next on my list was the lockbox key. Who had the key?

I came up with a plan. A plan I'd thought of before. I'd use my *Gazette* to draw out the key-holder. I spent all afternoon and night writing the article.

The next morning, I called Oneeda. "When can you come over to the *Gazette* and read tomorrow's lead story?"

Fifteen minutes later, she dropped the front-page story on my desk, her eyes wide as the buttons on her blouse. "I don't understand it. But whatever you've cooked up, I want in on it."

"Think about it," I said. "*The Gazette* will be in the hands of the movie crew tomorrow. Every one of them will read it. Freddie's killer will show up in Los Angeles with the key in a few days. You can count on it. I might even learn something new about Andrew's death."

THE GAZETTE

THE GAZETTE • TUESDAY, AUGUST 13, 1963

TULLULAH IVEY LOCKBOX REVEALS SECRETS

According to the Los Angeles District Attorney's office, the lockbox belonging to Tallulah Ivey contains evidence exonerating Mrs. Ivey in the shooting death of Rod Russell. Additional documents are said to contain evidence implicating illegal activities by a man closely associated with the actress's career.

The District Attorney would not return repeated phone calls. However the DA's office staff confirmed that the lockbox is still intact at City National Bank, until Mrs. Ivey is able to claim the contents during the continuing investigation.

There was more to the story, but it didn't matter for my purpose. This would be enough to coax out the key-holder. Next, I would have to convince Butch that we needed to be at that bank when the guilty party showed up.

I wrapped hot cornbread in tin foil, grabbed a bottle of JJ's Honey, and took off for the Sheriff's office.

He was pleased to see me.

Two days after the story appeared, Butch and I walked through the front door of the main branch of the Los Angeles City National Bank. We settled into separate, concealed locations. Me in the waiting area near the manager's desks, Butch observing from a glass-enclosed office. I kept a newspaper in my face. We waited.

Two Los Angeles detectives, male and female, were posing as tellers. They were in on the operation, and I felt safer for it.

Butch and I were probably wondering the same thing—*who would show up*? Would it be Carr? Goldsmith? Chinn? O'Brien? Tully Ivey, herself? Maybe Mastrioni?

The morning lingered into noon, then afternoon. I was hungry. Butch, likely starving.

By two-thirty, my stomach was growling. Butch paced inside the small office.

At three o'clock, the front door opened and I peeked over my newspaper. Tully Ivey entered. Only, this wasn't the Tully Ivey I remembered. She was in disguise, looking more like a homeless woman from the streets than a glittering movie star. A drab-colored scarf hid her red hair. I'd never seen her in any movie dressed like that.

I glanced over at Turnbull hiding behind the glass wall; he hadn't noticed Ivey enter the bank.

She walked to the cashier's cage, asked some questions, then walked back to sit near the main entrance. What the heck was she doing? Did she think she could waltz in here and claim the lockbox without a key? Maybe she had the key. Maybe she was waiting on somebody else to show.

I didn't have time to ponder my own question before Al Goldsmith opened the main door. Goldsmith?

Butch noticed him right away and stood. I hoped he wouldn't jump the gun and try to intercept him. Fortunately, Butch watched from his position.

Goldsmith wasted no time in addressing one of the desk managers. She seemed to know him. They exchanged smiles and words. She made a phone call, hung up, and escorted him to a door behind the teller counter. A man met them, and they disappeared through the door.

Butch came out from hiding and looked my way. Using the newspaper to shield myself from Ivey, I motioned for him to go back in the office and pointed toward the "homeless" woman. Butch stepped back into the office. I took a deep breath. All hunger pangs had vanished, replaced by adrenaline.

Randy Carr walked in and sat next to Ivey, their backs to the front windows. He hadn't bothered to dress in disguise. They didn't speak to each other; he just sat there, his head down. I could see her lips moving, telling him something.

Butch was watching them. He gave me a *thumbs up*. I had no idea what he was trying to tell me. Maybe it was time for us to go behind the teller counter, where Goldsmith had gone.

If Butch stepped out, I knew Ivey would see him and run. I put my palm out, motioning for him to stay put. He looked toward the bank entrance. Andy Chinn had entered.

Chinn? What the…? I peeked over my paper.

He was in a hurry, walking past Ivy and Carr to his right, not noticing them. Chinn walked directly to one of the manager's desks and showed her something in his hand. She smiled and escorted him through the same door Goldsmith had entered.

Butch came out from the tiny office. We looked at each other. I glanced towards Ivey. She spotted me. I had to either confront her, or go to the back, where Butch was headed. My decision was made when Ivey and Carr slipped out the front door. Butch and I met at the door behind the teller counter.

"What in the world's going on? They're all here," I said.

"Yep. Except for O'Brien and Mastrioni. Let's go."

The detectives followed us through the door.

Down a short corridor, a right turn, and twenty yards ahead—through a glass door—we saw Goldsmith and Chinn arguing. The banker was making a phone call. We rushed through the door to confront Goldsmith and Chinn.

Butch yelled, "Let's have it, Goldsmith."

"Have what?" His eyes were wide and angry.

"The key. Hand it over. You're under arrest."

"Andy has the key, not me," Goldsmith interrupted. "I'm here for the same reason you are. I *paid* for the lockbox and I want to know what's in it!"

Chinn tried to run, but the detectives quickly snatched him.

Butch addressed the two detectives. "Would y'all do us the honor of holding Mr. Chinn until we can have him extradited back to Mississippi?"

"You can't prove anything," Chinn blurted. "Just because I have the key doesn't mean I had anything to do with the shooting." He searched Butch's face, then mine, making his appeal. "It was *me* Tully wanted to shoot. Me! Not Dawkins. She had invited me to come over that night."

I grabbed Butch and pulled him to the side. "Have them hold him for Freddie's murder, not Dawkins's."

"What? How do you know?"

I turned to the detectives. "Take him in for the murder of Freddie Carpenter. We found the murder weapon—it was a teakettle. His fingerprints are on it."

Chinn froze. "It was an *accident*. He wasn't supposed to …" His voice trailed off as he realized he'd just confessed.

While the detectives handcuffed Chinn, Butch asked me, "How come I didn't know squat about the murder weapon?"

"We haven't exactly found it. But it's the only thing I could find missing from the post off—"

Chinn interrupted. "Wait! You just said my fingerprints were on it. You haven't found anything."

"What's important now is that you've confessed," I said. "Turn around."

I reached in both of his back pockets and found the letter from the California judge. I handed it to Butch. "As I was saying, Sheriff, the teakettle was the only thing I found missing from the post office."

"Now we know what to look for in the river," Butch said. "We'll find it." He beamed for the first time in a long time.

Turning his attention to the detectives, he said, "We'd appreciate it if you'd lock up these yahoos."

"Gladly," one of the detectives said.

Goldsmith yelled, "I haven't done anything wrong!"

"Maybe you haven't, but we're not about to let you go scot-free till we can sort this out," Butch said.

Chinn and Goldsmith were handcuffed, and the detectives about to escort them off when I said, "Oh, you should also arrest Tully Ivey."

"Whoa, wait a minute," the male detective said. "On what charge?"

"For the murder of Rod Russell."

"Say again?" the female detective said.

"She murdered Rod Russell, or rather, *had* him murdered."

Eyebrows pinched together, they stared at me, like they were waiting for an explanation.

"I'll explain later. Here's my card. Call me when you have her in custody."

"It doesn't work like that, Deputy. We'll have to speak with our chief first," the female detective said.

The male detective asked, "You do know who Tully Ivey is, don't you?"

"Oh, I know her very well. In fact, she was just here, in this very bank. She was in disguise. That's why you didn't recognize her. And if you have any gumption at all, you'll interview a Joanna Whitfield. She lives in West Hollywood." I reached in my purse for her number. "Here, write this down."

The detective pulled out his little pocket notebook and recorded the info. "What's this about?"

"The unsolved Rod Russell murder," I said. "Go be a hero. Capture the person responsible for *his* murder."

The detectives left with Chinn and Goldsmith in handcuffs.

The plan had worked. We had solved most of the puzzle, just not all of it.

Like how'd the note get in Dawkins's hand in the first place?

32
The Red Eye

Butch and I sat across the aisle from each other on the flight home. The plane's engines were so obnoxious, we had to talk a decibel louder.

"Martha, here we are, five hours from Memphis," he said. "You have plenty of time to explain why you think Tully Ivey wanted to shoot Chinn instead of Dawkins, and why she had this Russell fella murdered."

I laughed and said, "Well, it's just a theory. And I assure you, it won't take five hours. I'll start with the Dawkins shooting. One day, I was digging back over my notes—the notes I took all those times I interviewed Ivey and the crew. I came across something very interesting. In my first talk with her, she referred to Andrew and used the present tense. Not the past tense."

"I'm not following you," Butch said.

"Let me find my notes." I'd already explained my theory to Oneeda, but the Sheriff needed to hear it, too. I pulled the note pad from my purse and found the page. "Yep, here it is. Ivey said, 'Andrew knows I was innocent in the Russell shooting.' Why do you suppose she would use the present tense when she referred to Andrew? Her mind works like that. If she'd been thinking of Andrew Dawkins, she would have said, 'Andrew *knew* I was innocent.' She probably doesn't even believe in the afterlife. She had to be thinking of Andrew Chinn, the only Andrew alive. Not only that, but in the trial, she referred to Chinn as *Andrew* Chinn, not Andy. She always uses proper names, not nicknames. When you put all the pieces together, it makes sense."

"Whoa, wait a minute. It *doesn't* make sense." His forehead wrinkled into a puzzle.

"Think about it. Chinn was supposed to show up at her bedroom window. Ivey had invited *him*, not Andrew Dawkins. She typed both notes. She placed one note in the lockbox before coming to film the movie, and, much later, taped the other note to the window so Chinn would take it off and have it in his hands when she shot him. That's why the tape was on the front of the note—so it could be read from the outside. She was going to kill *Andrew Chinn*. She had placed the key on the ledge and wanted you to find it and open the lockbox. With Chinn dead, there would be no one to refute the note. She thought it would finally get the tabloids off her back for continuing to implicate her in the Russell killing. Randy Carr would use the note to stop them from running any more stories about her and Russell. Probably sue 'em for libel if they didn't stop."

"Oookay, go on," Butch said, drawing a breath, waving a hand for me to continue.

"Chinn must have arrived late that night, witnessed the shooting, and ran to Dawkins lying on the ground. He probably looked in the window, but didn't see Ivey. Maybe he saw the key on the ledge and took it. He never saw the note. That's why he didn't know what the key was for. Remember? He didn't learn about the lockbox until I ran the newspaper article in the *Gazette*. Chinn probably figured he needed to beat everybody to the bank. By then he must've figured out that Ivey had planned the whole thing. Whatever the lockbox contained was likely his meal ticket to blackmail Ivey. Remember, he never liked her anyway. He even told Goldsmith today at the bank that Ivey intended to shoot *him*. All the pieces fell together when he showed up with the key."

Butch ordered a bourbon from the stewardess. The first time I'd seen him drink alcohol. "What about Goldsmith? Why was he at the bank today? And Ivey?"

"Goldsmith probably figured there was something in the lockbox that could ruin his career. That article I wrote in the *Gazette*? It said a man was going to be implicated in some illegal activity. I was using that as bait. But we may never know what he's hiding."

"Do you think he had your Gazette burned?"

"I had two people in mind. At first, I thought it was the governor. But if you remember, Goldsmith trapped me into being an extra so he could discredit anything I wrote about the movie. If the movie had ever gotten made, there would be no way to stop the negative publicity. So, yes, I believe Goldsmith had my paper burned. Can't prove it, though."

Butch sipped on his bourbon. "Why'd Tully Ivey show up at the bank?"

"Because she had placed the note there herself. She probably wanted to make sure it got to the Los Angeles police. But she saw me and ran."

"Okay, but you remember what she told you that day in the car. Why'd she tell you those things? Wood said it was Ivey's motive for Dawkins's death."

"Think about it. She didn't admit to killing him. And you know yourself, it wasn't enough to bring a murder charge. The governor! He pressured Wood into bringing those charges to stop the movie production."

Holy Moses," Butch shouted, waking several sleepy people on the plane, "you could be right." A large population of bourbon entered his mouth.

I leaned across the aisle and whispered in his ear, "It's just a theory, Butch."

"All right. Go back to Freddie's murder. How did you know it was Chinn?"

"I didn't, not till he showed up with the key. I'm guessing he listened in on my phone conversation with Freddie about the California judge's subpoena. He went to the Greenlee post office to intercept the letter because he didn't want anybody knowing about it—not until he had time to get to Los Angeles and see the contents for himself. Freddie wouldn't let him take the letter. Chinn hit him with the teakettle, then buried him near the river... I feel horrible about Freddie. It's all my fault."

"Hogwash." He swallowed the last of his bourbon. "There's nothing else you could've done. You know, you could be right about all this."

"It's still a theory."

Butch produced a sly grin and said, "Well, here's a theory for you. The letter you tried to intercept from me—I could arrest you for that."

I leaned over and whispered, "Oh, but you won't, Butch Turnbull. You need me."

"I need your steak dinner," he said. "We had a bet. She was acquitted."

"I never said which conviction she'd receive. Our bet's still on. I think she'll be convicted on the Rod Russell murder."

"Okay. The bet's still on," he said, staring into an empty glass.

Now, all I had to do was get Tully Ivey's typewriter and the two notes, along with Joanna Whitfield's testimony, to the Los Angeles prosecutor's office. Surely they'd prosecute her.

To my mind, she had hatched a clever, evil plan. But would she get off in California, too? Many celebrities do. She'd lawyer-up with the best firm in Los Angeles, I was sure of it.

I sent everything to the Los Angeles prosecutor, talked on the phone with him for hours, even flew out—on their nickel—to meet.

Finally, on September sixteen, Butch and I flew back to the City of Angels. We met with the prosecutor to discuss our testimony—two days before the Rod Russell murder trial.

33
Justice

September 18, 1962. The Stanley Mosk Courthouse, Los Angeles.

It was a circus. Photographers were outside snapping photographs of the celebrities coming to see the trial. Tully Ivey had plenty of Hollywood friends. I recognized Gregory Peck, Sidney Poitier, Burt Lancaster, Jane Mansfield, Paul Neuman, and Bridgitte Bardot. More men than lady actors. No surprise there.

She entered the courtroom escorted by two guards. Her shoulders back, her chin held high, she exhibited no detectable guilt, or remorse.

I was called to the stand and spent an hour recounting the last year of my search for the truth. I told it all—everything I'd told Butch on the plane.

The prosecution then called Joanna Whitfield. Her lipstick was smeared above her lip line, her hair was a mess, and she had such bright blotches of red rouge on her cheeks that she almost looked comical. This could be a disaster.

The prosecution asked about her brother.

"Yes, he was a police officer. He was the first person at the scene. The restaurant manager told him that Tully Ivey had been there, having dinner with Rod Russell; but before they finished the meal, Tully Ivey had disappeared. It's all in the police records, probably buried in some old warehouse. My brother was found dead two months later. The restaurant manager is still missing."

Whew! She'd just recited the best lines of her acting career. I was proud of her. She had given a credible testimony.

Ivey's defense counsel frequently objected, but the judge overruled him.

The prosecution called Butch to the stand.

"Sheriff Turnbull, I'd like to hear your testimony going back to when you encountered Mr. Chinn and Mr. Goldsmith inside City National Bank. Tell this court what Mr. Chinn said when you confronted him."

Butch recounted Chinn's exact words. "He said, 'It was me she wanted to shoot. She put the note in the lockbox…'" Butch went on to tell everything about the encounter.

Ivey's lawyer objected again, trying to discredit Chinn's confession, but was overruled.

Butch continued to explain why it all made sense to him. He no longer referred to it as a theory. He told how Tully Ivey had planned it all from day one, before even coming to Mississippi. How she thought the note in the lockbox would exonerate her from the Rod Russell murder and put an end to the Hollywood tabloid stories. How she'd taped the note on the window, waiting for Andy—Andrew Chinn—to show up at midnight. How her plan all along was to murder him, leaving no one to refute the note in the lockbox.

“And she uses tarot cards,” Butch told the prosecutor.

“Did you find a tarot card in the lockbox?”

“Yes, sir. The Devil card. I suppose she thought nobody would believe she’d leave the Devil card to herself.”

In cross-examination, Ivey’s attorney said, “Good story, Sherriff. But you have no proof, do you? Just theories.” He faced the jury. “I hope the intelligent people of California will keep in mind the difference between a theory and cold hard facts. Sheriff Turnbull’s story is simply a story, nothing more.”

The prosecution continued with witnesses and testimony about the night Russell was murdered. Besides Joanna Whitfield’s testimony, the prosecution presented her brother’s report as evidence. The report spelled out the restaurant manager’s account of what she’d seen—Tully Ivey leaving the table and not returning when two gunmen stepped into the restaurant and shot Russell.

Four police officers testified, each recounting what Joanna’s brother had told them.

When the prosecutor rested his case, I thought Tully Ivey would survive another murder trial. I’d probably go home in a funk.

The defense tried to make her look like a saint. Then he rested his case.

During closing arguments the next day, the prosecution and the defense delivered impassioned pleas, the prosecution for a conviction, the defense for acquittal.

The prosecution reminded the jury of the police report putting Ivey at the scene the night Russell was murdered—even speculating that two of Pileggi's men had pulled the trigger. While Ivey's lawyer continued to remind the jury there were no eyewitnesses that could testify.

The judge instructed the jurors to deliberate and return with a verdict. Surely, it would be a difficult decision for them.

Outside the courtroom, I told Butch, "I don't think there's enough evidence to convict her. I'll probably be buying you a steak dinner. Just make it cheap."

The jury deliberated for four days, while Butch and I didn't know what to do. We visited museums and took a tour of MGM's lot. Mostly, we remained glum.

The daily front-page newspaper stories did nothing to assuage our doubts about any conviction.

One gossip columnist even wrote, "Tully Ivey on trial for murder? It can't be true!"

I kept telling Butch, "She'll be free as a bird."

On the fifth morning, Butch received a call in his hotel room. The jury was ready to render their verdict.

"All rise!" the bailiff bellowed.

"Has the jury determined a verdict?" the Los Angeles judge asked the foreman.

"We have, Your Honor. We, the jury, find the defendant guilty as charged."

I couldn't help myself. I gave Butch a hug. "It's no longer a theory, is it?"

"Nope," Butch said, grinning.

"I never thought they'd convict her without an eyewitness."

"The police report was convincing," he said.

Walking out of the courtroom, I said, "I'd like my steak dinner at Lusco's."

"Lusco's? No way. Too expensive."

"Take it out of petty cash. You've earned it. So have I.

On the plane ride home, I asked Butch, "Whadda you think'll happen to Goldsmith?"

"We'll probably never pin your *Gazette* fire on him. But, hey, he lost his movie. He lost all his money."

"What about the rest of the bunch?"

"Looks like Mastrioni and O'Brien did nothing wrong. Tully Ivey is going to prison. Randy Carr won't likely be charged with anything. And then, there's Chinn."

"I believe he'll live to see another day," I said. "Until you can find that teakettle. Probably won't be convicted unless you do."

"I know, Martha, I know. Somewhere in the Yazoo River."

We remained silent until he leaned across the aisle and said, "You know, you kinda have a knack for this police work. I just might promote you to detective. Maybe. Some day."

I leaned back and closed my heavy eyelids.

After we landed, I headed for Solo, but stopped at Shirley's house first.

She came to the door. I handed her Andrew's old typewriter. We hugged.

"Martha, thank you. You did it."

"Did what?"

"You found out the truth. I guess I was just naïve about Andrew's cheating. I don't think that was the first time."

"I'm sorry."

"Please, come in and sit."

"Thank you, but I really need to run. I have a story to write. But look, I want you to come to supper at my place, once a week. Will you promise me?"

She could only nod and wipe away a tear.

I walked in the front door of my house as Father Paul was walking out—with Mary and little Michael.

"Mary! You're back!" I leaned down to hug Michael. "And

with my favorite little boy."

"You knew I couldn't stay away long," Mary said.

I smiled, knowing she must've heard about Chinn's arrest. I turned to Father Paul.

"Y'all headed to church?"

"No, we're going to teach Michael a lesson," he said.

"A lesson?"

"Yep. We're going to the Grater house to look for Tully Ivey's tarot cards."

"I'm going with you."

Father Paul was quick to respond. "Martha, would you mind taking Mary and Michael in your car? After this, I'm driving to Parchman for a Bible study."

"Of course. Oh, wait, let me see if Chinn left any cards."

Mary and Michael climbed in my car while I hustled upstairs and searched Chinn's old room. I found a tarot deck in his bedside table, next to the Bible I always kept in my boarders' rooms. I stuffed them both in my purse and headed for my car.

I followed Father Paul to the Grater house. Ten minutes later, we knocked on an unlocked door. No one was home. I led them to the library. On the side table beside the wingback chair were several cards laid out in neat rows.

Father Paul gathered them up, and we followed him outside. He found a spot in the backyard and tossed the cards in a pile. "Michael," he said, "you are never to play with these kind of cards. Remember these pictures. Your mother doesn't ever want you playing with them. Do you understand?"

Michael was six years old. He stared at the cards and nodded.

I opened the Bible and flipped to 2 Chronicles 33, and pointed to the verse. "Here, Paul, why don't you read some of this."

He began to read, "'Manasseh was twelve years old when he began to reign, and he reigned fifty-five years in Jerusalem. He used fortune-telling and omens and sorcery, and dealt in mediums. He did much evil in the sight of the LORD, provoking him to anger.'"

He closed the Bible and handed it back to me.

Mary knelt beside her son. "The father is right, Michael. Never ever touch these kinds of cards."

Father Paul reached in his pocket and retrieved a box of matches. He knelt and lit the pile of cards. We watched in amazement as the ink melted into grotesque images of evil.

Riding back into Solo, Mary asked, "Did you know somebody's building a new cotton gin in Solo?"

"I forgot to tell you," I said. "Shirley called. Seems Andrew left her with a good bit of life insurance money. She's going in with some other farmers to build a gin. Right next to the juke joint."

"I'm happy for her," Mary said.

Little Michael was curious. "What's a juke joint, Aunt Martha?" He was beginning to think of me as his aunt.

"We'll, sweetie, it's a place where Black folks can get together and listen to the blues, socialize, and dance."

"What's the blues?" he wanted to know.

I looked over at Mary. She was smiling. She answered him. "The blues is a kind of music that comes from here in the Delta. It can be sad, and it can be fun."

Michael seemed satisfied.

I declared, "One Saturday night, I'm gonna walk straight into that joint and listen to the blues. I don't care what anybody says."

"I don't need to go. I can hear it from my window," Mary said.

The next week, Oneeda, Mary, and I sat in the parlor. When the cuckoo clock struck five, I opened a bottle of sherry.

Pouring each of us a glass, I said, "The governor's office contacted me. They want to throw some sort of party in my honor at the mansion. The chief-of-staff even sent me a full-length purple gown from Kenington's. The note said the governor's wife picked it out."

"Let's see it," a jubilant Oneeda said.

I retrieved the dress from my room. Holding it up, I asked, "Do you think it's too low-cut? Looks like there's going to be some cleavage showing."

"No," Oneeda assured me.

"Absolutely not," Mary offered. "When is it?"

“December twenty first, and you’re both invited,” I said, smiling.

“You know what?” Oneeda said. “Nobody ever explained how the governor was mixed up in this business—his lockbox and all.”

“I’ll explain it,” I said. “It was pure coincidence.”

“You should be ashamed,” Mary said. “When did you start believing in coincidences?”

“Oh, my goodness, I don’t,” I said, laughing at myself. “You’re so right. What was I thinking? It was providential. The governor was the turning point.”

“Exactly,” Oneeda said. “If you hadn’t gotten the governor involved, that movie would’ve been made and the whole world would think we’re just a bunch of—a bunch of—what’d you call it, Martha?”

“Heathens. Blood-thirsty ignorants.” I raised my wine glass with theirs, and we tinkled them together. “Yep. And do y’all believe it’s true, what Father Paul said?”

“What did he say?” Mary asked.

“He said, ‘Shallow people believe in luck. Worldly people believe in coincidence. God-fearing people believe in providence.’”

They agreed, and we sipped more sherry.

Oneeda chimed in. “Since God knows all and is *just* in all his ways, I’m sure he knows about the four-dollar bet we made. Both of you owe me four dollars.”

"But our bet was for the Dawkins trial," I said.

"Not really," Oneeda said. "The bet was Ivey would go to jail. And I won."

"Well, God's also merciful, and he knows I don't have four dollars," I said. "So you'll have to rely on his *love*."

"What? You're gonna welch on the bet?"

Mary and I laughed as we opened our purses and handed eight dollars to Oneeda.

"Now you'll have to treat us to lunch at Charlie's Place," Mary said.

"Now all has been heard;
here is the conclusion of the matter:
Fear God and keep his commandments,
for this is the whole duty of man.
For God will bring every deed into
judgment, including every hidden thing,
whether it is good or evil."

— Ecclesiastes 12:13, 14

THE ACTRESS

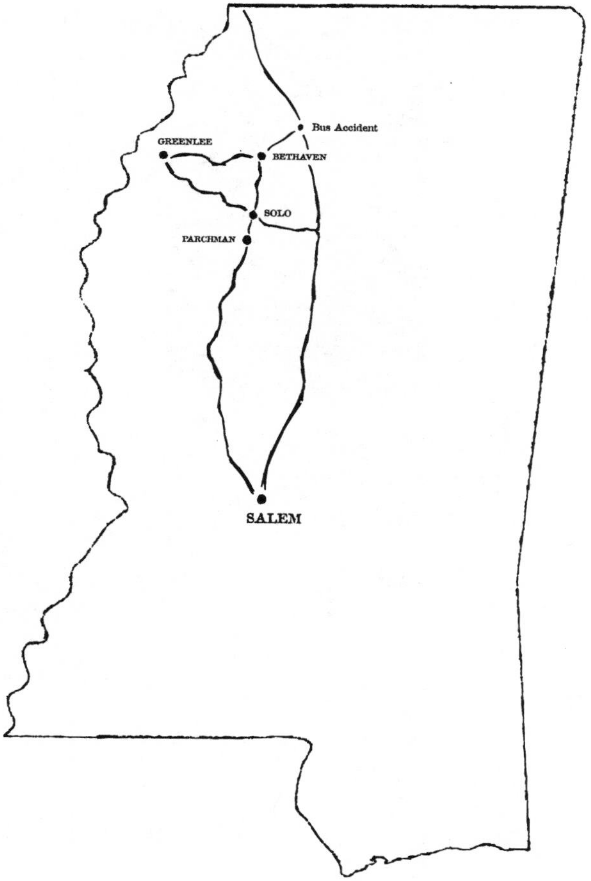

Bus Accident
GREENLEE
BETHAVEN
SOLO
PARCHMAN
SALEM

About the Author

MICHAEL HICKS THOMPSON was born in his mother's own bed. Raised on a small farm in Mississippi, he claims to know a thing or two about strong Christian women, alcoholic men, and Jesus. He graduated from Ole Miss, served in the military, then received a master's degree in mass communication from the University of South Carolina. Married to Tempe Adams for forty-five years, he lives in Memphis, Tennessee. He's the father of three Christian men, and grandfather of four. The little ones call him "Big Mike."

For more information on the author and his books, visit: **http://www.michaelthompsonauthor.com**. Be sure to sign up for his monthly *"Stay Up With Mystery!"* newsletter. Free mystery topics, free books, free fun.

Next in the *Solo* series.

You haven't met my sister, Florine Hicks. She came to stay with me. Before you learn about her, you should know why she came. Her husband, Peter, was dying. She needed to get away for a few days. That's how it started.

In the Delta, we usually tell all, but I'm gonna spare you from the spoiler. No sense spoiling the story for you. You'll just have to read about my sister, Peter, the Sheriff, the murder, and all that happened in our tiny place of good dirt and rich stories; because the Mississippi Delta has always been a mysterious place, full of zestful people and liquid conversation.

Also by Michael Hicks Thompson:

The Rector (first in the *Solo* series)

DAVID — The Illustrated Novel, Volume I

DAVID — The Illustrated Novel, Volume II

Dinner with David ben Jesse (*Dinner with Destiny,* anthology from Amazing Phrase Publishing)

The Parchman Preacher (replaced by *The Rector*)

The Sister (due for release in 2017)

Clouds Above (due for release in 2017)

If you enjoyed The Actress, please leave a comment on Amazon, next to the book. Amazon will promote the book once 200 comments and star ratings have been entered.

Made in the USA
Charleston, SC
29 January 2017